WEIRD & WONDERFUL

10 Short Stories

Neil Kilby

For Carol

CONTENTS

INSIGHTS

1. I've Got a Gun (The Friendly Assassin)
Hands are probably the most amazing tools in the world. Is it possible that by using our imagination, they could be so much more?

2. The White Walls Room
Art galleries are wonderful places to sit in, to see and feel, or maybe even dream of what the artist was trying to share, then to be drawn into their world.

3. Bruce and Julia
There's something perfect about cats. That's what they want us to believe. Who are we to deny such superiority?

4. Five Ghosts
What if the spirits that are between this life and the next are given another chance? Could redemption be earned if they saved someone teetering on the brink?

5. Happy Birthday x
Living alone with a dog called Scat, Patricia takes to the countryside a few days before her birthday. Will her life change beyond her own imagining.

6. Quirk-Keys
You know what it's like when you lose your keys, so can you imagine what would happen if you can't find them?

I'VE GOT A GUN

(The Friendly Assassin)

Jon woke with the cold realisation that this was another work-day. His head hurt, not just from the headaches he had been suffering from, but also from the thought of having to go to work in a job he was bored with.

He moved his head gently towards the crack of light that was appearing around his blackout blind. A few more minutes and movement would be necessary, but he held on to the thought - warm bed or the cold bedroom? He slipped his legs over the edge of the bed.

His heating rarely worked, so he put on some socks and a dress-ing gown quickly, to keep warm. First thing he did was to put on his small electric fire, to take the edge off the room. He reached towards the window blind and pulled it up. Wiping the conden-sation off the window, he surveyed the rows of back-to-back gardens, cobbled together fences, clothes lines that poked up here and there, some with washing on, probably inadvertently left overnight, some obviously left on and completely forgotten about, going greyer by the day.

A dull, damp mist caressed all the buildings softening the bleak landscape. This did not improve Jon's mind; autumn had taken hold of his thoughts and feelings.

It's fair to say that the mindset in this situation brings about more darkness, but somehow the reality of life is to move forward, whether it's ambition or just the need to survive, you just have to keep going.

Because he was on the top floor, he had a better view over this suburban vista and, as he stared out, he felt convinced that he was not the only one whose life seemed to be going nowhere.

He considered momentarily to sum up his life. At the moment, out of ten, he felt his life was about three and a half; the half being the optimist in him.

He made coffee, sat and drank it slowly, felt the rumble of the inter-city train as it gained speed. Then it zipped past the end of the row of terraced houses, the only blessing being he couldn't see it. It would sometimes keep him awake, but then at other times it would lull him off to sleep.

He ate some toast whilst he surveyed his rented abode. It was decorated quite well in traditional magnolia with a few posters across the walls, some of favourite bands he'd been to see. One big poster which he loved was across the main wall, above his old brown leather settee - a full colour photo of New Zealand, a place he wanted to go to. Somehow this always cheered him up.

On the wall by the kitchen units, there was a small group of family photos. His mum and dad, both now passed away, his sister whom he hadn't seen in years, mainly because she lived up north. He had texts from her now and again asking him to visit her, her husband and the three kids. She would say, "You are an uncle three times over! Come and see them!" He'd make excuses: work, time, illness.

He promised himself - maybe next year. He sent them money for Christmas. They sent each other Christmas and birthday cards. This is how it went. "Families" and "keeping in touch" are sometimes just words.

The flat he lived in was just one room that covered the loft area of the house. Jon was lucky. Most of the flats in the building were less than half the size of his. Fortunately, it also had a toilet, so he didn't have to share. The bathroom, however, he did have to share. That was another story.

Jon, being now in his mid-thirties, could feel the pull of all these things in his head; missed opportunities at work and relationships which had slipped by.

In the recent past, he had had girlfriends who wanted to mould him to their thoughts. He had been stubborn, but perhaps he had never really fallen in love.

He wasn't bad-looking - nearly six foot tall, slim, fair-haired, the sort of face that was more soft than rugged. So, more often than not, because he was a lazy person, he had a beard, which suited him.

As far as work was concerned, he was a manager of a betting shop, which gave him enough money to pay for his flat, go out with the few friends most weekends, go to see bands. He hadn't got a car, but he could drive. He had a bicycle that he used when he got into a health kick. Now, he was at a hiatus; in other words, too much weight, but no enthusiasm to starve himself.

He had a small amount of savings that he hoped would give him the exotic holiday he'd longed for. He was waiting for the right moment.

Most of his friends were paired off, having kids or about to do so. Now he was beginning to feel a bit isolated. He looked up through the roof window. The day was still grey. He moved across to the sink. Above this was a small window which looked down on a side garden, then another house with an electricity pylon, whose power line drooped across to the next post. On this sat a pigeon. It looked asleep.

Jon was sure this was the same pigeon that sat on the chimney each night and continuously cooed all evening. Last night it kept him awake, even after the headache had subsided. The noise travelled down the chimney and came out through the fireplace. Despite now being defunct, it still produced an echo. Jon looked at the pigeon and said,

"You noisy arsehole, you kept me awake most of the night!"

Maybe it was a slight exaggeration, but Jon wasn't in the best of moods.

He tapped the window. The pigeon didn't move a muscle. More abuse was welling up inside Jon. He made his hand into the shape of a gun, then pulled back his thumb just like he used to do when he was a kid, when he pretended to be a cowboy.

He made a bang sound. It was strange. It was almost as if time stood still. Then, in slow motion, a second passed. Suddenly, the pigeon exploded like a powder puff, as thousands of feathers floated into the air and then found their way slowly to the ground.

The pigeon, now free from his feathers, sat there almost as if it was waiting to be placed on a barbecue, then it slowly swung around on the wire and was now left hanging upside down on the power line, just a simmering corpse. Smoke gently rose from its carcass and mixed strangely with the morning mist.

Jon looked at his clenched hand, immediately released it, looked again at the pigeon and, for one moment, thought it was he who had committed this poor beast to an early grave. To be honest, it looked like it might be hanging there for some time to come.

He gathered his now racing thoughts and started to rationalise them. Being a betting man, he wondered what the odds were. A pigeon being electrified at the exact time as someone pretending to shoot it. He quickly guessed at a million to one. Perhaps today was the best day to place a bet then, but he was no fool.

Jon thought that maybe a worn wire ended its perpetual cooing. After all this, Jon got ready, just briefly pausing to look out of the window at the now dripping, damp body of the pigeon.

He opened his front door and made his way down four flights of stairs. At the bottom, he could hear pop music coming from one of the flats.

Close to the communal kitchen, a door was open. This flat belonged to Mr. Kulikovski, better known as The Duke. His room was a third of the size of that of Jon. On one wall, a big flat-screen TV continually played pop videos, for which he had a fascination. Although Jon had his own kitchen, he sometimes used the communal one, if he was lonely and needed to talk.

The Duke was there most the time, usually leaving his flat door open. Sometimes, Jon could hear him singing along to the music or he'd even be dancing, "dad dancing", occasionally taking a female tenant waltzing up and down the hall! The enjoyment was often mutual. Needless to say, he was a charmer.

He was smaller than Jon but seemed taller in some strange way. He had a hard to explain stature, a personality larger than life itself. With a permanent goaty beard, a moustache that turned upwards at the ends, that he waxed, short grey hair, he was rugged but good-looking; the kind of face that made you like him immediately. He looked smart yet he was always casually dressed. Jon could never work out how he looked so good, despite living in such small accommodation. Jon always thought it must be in his genes and coming from such a cold country,

"Hullo!" said The Duke. "Hi!" replied Jon. He loved his accent so much that he would ask him about his life whenever he could.

The Duke had told Jon that he lived in St Petersburg when he was a child, then moved around Russia with his parents, who, according to him, were always being persecuted for being related to the Russian royal family.

He would say that his grandparents and then his parents searched for many years for the proof that would change their standing in the community. After some time, they were moved on by the communists, so they left Russia, ending up in Britain.

He was now alone. He had said to Jon he was 79 but looked and acted like a much younger man. His parents had died many years ago, now it was up him to trace his family's roots. Maybe one day he would, if he had the money. Whether this was true or not, it mattered little. Everyone knew Mr. Kulikovski as The Duke.

He was superb at making coffee. Jon wasn't certain what he put in it, because he would never tell him, but Jon was sure it was vodka and/or some illegal substance. Either way, Jon always had one just before he left for work and it always gave him a spring in his step.

"See you later, Duke! Have a good one!"

"Hope you have a good day too", The Duke would say, with that accent that made Jon think of winter nights and burning log fires and maybe a Russian princess to keep him warm.

Jon would catch the bus to work at around about half past nine. It was only a short trip to the common, where Jon would get off and walk to the shop. He stood in the bus queue. A rag-and-bone bunch of people would be there, young kids on their way to the job centre or to go shoplifting in the town. This was perhaps Jon's jaundiced point of view, but he hadn't got time to think anything better of them. They were mixed with a few doddering old-age pensioners. This usually caused grief when the older people would start grumbling about how badly-behaved the youth were today and the young people would swear at them, which would make the whole thing go off.

Today it was relatively quiet but, just before Jon was about to climb on board the bus, a cyclist glanced against him, almost knocking him over. As he was riding on the pavement, the boy fell off his bike onto the grass by the bus stop. He immediately got up and squared up to Jon; a funny sight, as he reached all the way up to Jon's chest in height!

Jon looked down at him, but the boy turned back, crest-fallen, to pick up his bike, grabbed it, then sent a string of expletives Jon's way. This amused all the young people in the bus queue. With equal measure, the old people moaned about it.

Jon merely felt ill at ease with it. He climbed on the bus, went upstairs and sat on the back seat. He had fifteen minutes between stops, so time to think, but before he knew it, the bus was passing the young lad on the bike. Jon was amused by this and knocked the window to get his attention, then made a v sign in the lad's direction. Being parallel to the bus, the lad looked up and made the same gesture back at Jon. This annoyed Jon, so he held up his right hand like a gun, as he had done with the pigeon, pulled his thumb and made as if to pull the trigger and said, "Bang!"

Jon was staggered to see the wheels on the bike come off, as the boy crashed to the floor. Jon saw that he could clearly have broken a few bones, as the bus slowed for a second. Jon felt really satisfied and then looked at his hand, studying it, gently releasing it from the shape of a gun. Jon felt strange, his head felt fuzzy, like he had had a few drinks. He wasn't sure what was happening, if anything at all, but somehow it had lifted his mind about the grey day.

Jon got off the bus and began to walk across the common. This was the time to think. He began to feel strange, as if he had some sort of supernatural power. With his hands wedged into his jacket pockets, Jon was lost in his thoughts.

He was awoken from them by a dog, snuffling round his feet. Jon looked down. It was a sort of spaniel cross, all brown and like a small bear. He leant down to pat it. The dog paused briefly, wagged its tail, looked up at Jon, wagged its tail again, enthusiastically, then ran off quickly.

The day had lightened. As Jon walked, a tinge of autumn sunshine graced the almost leafless trees. Underfoot, the recent stormy weather had left piles of multicoloured leaves sitting randomly against bushes, trees and fences.

Jon felt his mood lift considerably. He kicked the leaves as he walked, feeling somewhat like a child who had discovered so many things in one day and didn't know what to do with them.

He was disturbed slightly from his juvenile thoughts, as he found the same dog jumping around in the leaves with him. He thought this was wonderful, in the day that had started on a score close to three and a half and was now nearing six and a half.

Then things got even better, as he heard the owner of the little dog shouting loudly behind him to try and control it. "Bach, Bach, stop, stop, sit!"

Jon immediately stopped, as if he was the one who was required to do so.

"Sorry!" said the voice. "So sorry! He's usually more docile than this!"

Jon lifted his head only slightly, almost as if the teacher from his school was chastising him for being naughty. He looked up slowly; with some of the leaves that were hanging in the air, added to the autumn sunshine directly behind the voice, he knew somehow that this was a special moment.

He was silent. The voice was turning into a face as the young woman walked around in front of him. She couldn't stop apologising in one way or another. She stopped for a moment, he gathered his thoughts, she collared the dog and started to walk away, then, as if someone had gifted speech back to a dumb man, he spoke.

"It's ok, no problem."

As she walked away, she said, "By the way, the dog's name is like the composer. Silly, I know, but I like it."

Now he could see her face clearly. She smiled beautifully, her short auburn hair glistening in the autumn sun, her small, perfectly-formed oval face, her glacial blue eyes, lips that you could be forever lost in.

Jon tried to gather his thoughts. He wanted to call after her, as she walked away, but for some reason the words never came. He felt rooted to the ground; when he looked again, she was gone.

Jon was angry. He let out a cry of anguish, then thought, "Why didn't I get her number or even fuss the dog?" He sat on a nearby bench to console himself.

Now he knew that he would forever walk the common at this time every day, until he found that angel again.

The remarkable thing was, previously, he had had no time for dogs, but he had fallen in love with Bach as well.

A squirrel was burying nuts in the ground under a tree nearby. Jon watched, thinking lovingly of the girl, then, almost playfully, without thinking of earlier, he made a gun shape with his hand, pulled back his thumb and ...

"Bang!"

The squirrel looked towards him, then, a second later, disappeared up the big tree. It dawned on Jon that the squirrel didn't die, fall down or blow up, just harmlessly escaped. As he got up and prepared to walk along the footpath, he heard a rustling noise up above. He looked up, only to find the squirrel skimming past his nose onto the floor. He could swear he heard it squeak but it was as dead as dead can be.

Jon panicked, full of fear, and ran as fast as he could all the way to the shop. It was only a few hundred yards away now. He then stopped, rested his hands on his knees, started to breathe more evenly and thought to himself,

"What am I running away from? I can't run away from myself!"

He then walked slowly to Thebettshop, whose name sat above it in white and red letters. Jon opened the front door to the betting shop, situated between a charity shop and a pound shop; the perfect place, some might say.

Jon felt relieved normality, thinking about work and the beautiful girl he'd just met.

He started by pinning up the racing pages on the boards. It was an old-fashioned betting shop, so technology and gaming machines were not part of the fittings. However, it still made good profits, so, for now, his job was safe. He knew the shop was soon to have a big refit so who could tell what the future might bring? Regulars straggled in. The usual suspects, most of whom he knew, of course, but occasionally, the odd man or woman would come in and place some way-out bet that either worked or failed dismally, mostly the latter. The morning went quite quickly, so no time to think on his morning revelations. His assistant took over while he went onto the high street for lunch. Now the watery sun was warming roofs, walls and benches. A soft white mist was hanging here and there, so he sat in the square to eat a sandwich.

There was a wooden seat that wrapped around a large sculpture. It had anodised metal strips of varying lengths that curled towards the now bluing sky. Entangled in these metal strips there was a mermaid of sorts, with her hands stretched towards the sun. He was never sure what it represented because, where he lived, you couldn't get any further from the sea, but as he looked up, the mermaid looked so much like the angel he had met in the park. He watched people moving around the shopping centre, as he finished his high-priced luxury coffee.

He thought about the things that had shaped his day, realising he could most probably explain away the episodes this morning. His mind, however, was consumed by the girl. He tried to see her face in his mind's eye; he guessed late twenties, so at least she was near his age. He tried to think if there had been a wedding ring, but no, he couldn't remember. He did recall thinking she was about his height, as he had been able to look straight into her eyes.

Then his thoughts skipped back to the pigeon, faulty-electric-wire-dead pigeon. Young kid on badly maintained bike; he WAS an idiot, his own fault. The squirrel? His best thought was there must have been some child-with-a-catapult, so, dead squirrel. Somehow, he still felt uneasy about it though.

He looked down at his hand, made it into the shape of a gun, immediately changed it and mumbled to himself, "Stupid!"

Back at the betting office, he made himself comfortable behind the desk and took a couple of paracetamol, as his head was aching again. He reminded himself that he should drink less caffeine.

There was no real security in the shop, just a low piece of glass between him and the customers. There were more customers than usual, because of the big race later. As Jon worked through all the betting slips, he heard a familiar voice. Mr. Kulikovski was making his way towards the counter, exchanging pleasantries with other regulars. When he got to the counter, The Duke said,

"Hi Jon! You doing ok today?"

Jon replied,

"Yeah, fine! Not seen you in here for a while!"

"You know me, Jon! I only spend my money when there is a certainty," he said with a glint in his eye.

"Oh!" said Jon, "Not sure that anything is certain."

The Duke leaned forward and whispered,

"On this beautiful day, there is love in the air and I have a horse that will win!"

He pushed the betting slip towards Jon, who looked at it and whispered back,

"This is a rank outsider, Duke!"

"I know," replied The Duke, "but it is a name attached to my family! It will win!"

He pushed a hundred pounds towards Jon. It was a hundred to one, on a horse called Alexandria. He passed the slip back to The Duke, who then slipped it into his pocket. The Duke smiled. Jon smiled. Jon wanted The Duke to win but thought there's nothing he could do to make it happen, but he looked The Duke in eye and winked. Jon made a gesture with his hand, inadvertently, and said,

"It could go "bang" and win!"

For a second, Jon thought nothing of it; after all it was just a gesture, something he did often, but then his thoughts were doing somersaults. As Jon reflected on the day, in the few seconds it was taking to process it, The Duke's face turned white. He gripped his chest and collapsed to the floor.

The wait was agonising. In the ambulance on the way to the hospital, Jon apologised continuously. Unfortunately, The Duke was out cold, and the paramedics were struggling to keep him alive.

When they got to the hospital, Jon was asked,

"Are you a relative?"

He thought for a second, knowing that The Duke had no-one, so he said,

"Yes, I'm his son."

He wasn't sure why he said it; maybe he always thought it would be great to have a father like The Duke.

After what seemed like ages, Jon was on his way to the ward, sipping another coffee. He opened the door to intensive care, where he found The Duke, wires leading everywhere. A doctor spoke to Jon.

"Your father is lucky! A minute later he would not have made it."

As he was sitting next to The Duke's bed, Jon's mind wandered away to the park, thinking about the angel he had met earlier in the day.

He was absent-mindedly staring out of the window into the darkness. The bright lights of the ward had a strange effect, as they tried to balance with streetlights outside. Then, like an apparition, he could see her in the window; the beautiful face was there, in front of him. It was only when he heard her voice from inside the room that he realised it was her reflection that he could see.

Jon turned slowly and stared at the girl. Quickly, he asked, "What's your name? What's your phone number?"

She hesitated. "Olivia, nurse Olivia. Are you ok?" She paused, then added, "Aren't you the guy from the park this morning?"

He said, "Yes!"

Then Jon realised how strange he must have sounded and started to explain what had happened to Mr. Kulikovski.

She listened and said,

"Would you like a coffee? I have a break in ten minutes."

They were sat in the staff canteen, Jon opposite Olivia. She said, "So he's not your dad?"

"No, he's a neighbour of mine who lives in the same set of flats. I've known him for a few years. He has no family. Anyway, it's my fault."

"Why is it your fault?" asked Olivia.

"He has had a heart attack, yes, but I shot him!"

"What!" cried Olivia.

"I shot him in the betting office where I work."

Olivia wanted to speak but listened, as Jon started his story about the day. The pigeon, the boy, meeting her, the squirrel, and Mr. Kulikovski. There seemed to be a warm haze over them both, as Jon divulged his tale. As he reached the end of his account, they were holding hands across the table, in pleasant silence. Olivia then said,

"Your eyes are very bloodshot. Do you feel ok?" He replied,

"No, I have a terrible headache."

Then he continued,

"It's because of this thing with my hand."

He looked at it and smiled.

"How crazy am I? How can a hand kill, just shaped like a gun?".

He swung his hand around and pointed at his own head, as if in a gesture of fun. He then said. "Bang!" and collapsed to the floor.

There was darkness. He could hear sounds; voices, they came and went. There was a grey haze that looked like clouds. He thought he saw angels or was it just one? They all had the same face, but he couldn't focus.

Olivia's face was somewhere in his head. He thought this must be heaven but surely you can see things in heaven.

There was a light. It got stronger. He could see shapes, he could hear things more clearly, his eyes opened, more words came towards him, almost too many. The first face he saw was The Duke's, whose smile was unmistakable.

Jon focused on the room as the Duke spoke. It was the same intensive care room that the Duke was in.

"Yes! There you are my friend!" said The Duke. "Back with the living. It's a strange place, I know, but no stranger than where you have been. In fact, it's a club somewhere between the dead and the living. We have been there, you and me. We know."

Jon said one word, "Olivia", in a broken, very quiet voice. The Duke replied, "It's ok, she's here."

Olivia appeared at the side of the bed in her nurse's uniform. "She has been looking after you, my friend. She is a goddess!"

With this, Olivia's face went bright red, and she said,

"This man is a charmer and a lovely man!"

Now it was The Duke's turn to colour up.

"My dear friend, here is some coffee in a flask," he whispered.

"This will hit the spot! Take it slowly!"

Jon managed to give his first smile. The Duke stood up.

"By the way, my horse Alexandra came in first! I won ten thousand pounds! It was a good day after all!"

Another smile broke out on Jon's face. The Duke shook his hand, saying "See you soon, my son!" and then winked at him. As he left the room, Jon waved.

Olivia sat by the side of the bed and held his hand.

"It's ok, Jon. You had an aneurism, a blood clot. We put you into a coma. You've been out for three weeks."

He looked at this vision of loveliness, thought carefully and knew this was right. Her eyes told him so. There were thousands of words in his head, but his mouth was almost redundant. Olivia then said, "There's so much time! Don't worry about talking until you're feeling better."

The only words that came out of his mouth were,

"Have you ever been to New Zealand?"

She said, "No, but if you're asking me, we can go when you're better".

As days go, this had definitely turned into a nine and the optimist in him gave it a ten.

There was an irritating sound in the darkness. Jon opened his eyes. After a long sleep he was now in a normal ward to recover. He focused on the sound. It was a fly that he suspected was looking for winter hibernation. Jon looked around the room. It was very still. All the other patients seemed sound asleep. He looked down at his hand, made the shape of a gun. He took aim, pulled back his thumb and said,

"Bang.."

The fly crashed to the ground. Jon moved his index finger towards his mouth, blew some imaginary smoke from the end of his finger, then went back to sleep.

THE WHITE WALLS ROOM

1 The beautiful woman

The gallery had many rooms, with many paintings, in many styles.

One room in the gallery was large and painted white, with enough space to hang one painting on each wall, so it gave the maximum impact. In the middle of the room, there was a white block bench to sit on. The floor was made of beautiful, old, polished oak. In the centre of each wall, there was a painting. A spotlight shone on each one. Even so, the lighting was subdued. The bench was square, so you could sit on any side of it, to relax and view a painting of your choice.
The paintings were modern, but you could discern what each one might be about.

It was lunchtime. A beautiful young woman walked into the white walls room. She sat pertly on the white bench. A paper bag that she had with her was placed by her side, whilst her handbag lay on the other side. She slid her hand into the paper bag, pulling out a banana, which she delicately relieved of its skin and then ate, slowly and correctly.

The woman was in her thirties. Her demeanour gave off an air of confidence. She could have been a PA, a magazine editor, a scientist; she looked so good, maybe even a model.

The woman's phone beeped with a text message. She took it from her bag, scrolled down the messages, smiled to herself, then texted a reply and smiled again. In her eyes there could be seen a look of self- satisfaction, then she pulled out an envelope from her handbag, held some photographs that were inside, before going through them. She looked around to make sure there was no-one else in the room, even checking to see if there were any CCTV cameras.

She looked at one of the photographs, showing a man lying naked on a bed, holding a woman in a sexual embrace. The man's face could clearly be seen, but not the woman's. The woman was her. Her mind slipped back to that night and the pleasurable feeling of having sex with a famous person, but now the pleasure would be to make the man pay, or the photographs would end up in the media, destroying his reputation as well as that of his family.

She slipped her phone and the photographs back into her bag.

This beautiful woman sat serenely. She had an agenda; after all this was her job. She wore a red dress, red shoes, and a small black jacket.

It was warm in the room, so, after drinking her shop-bought latte, she slipped off her jacket and lay it next to her bag, before standing up. Now feeling more comfortable, she wandered around the room, stopping to take in each of the paintings. A thought came into her head, "Now, I might just get into the market for an expensive piece of art." Her thoughts were racing, then she stopped at one of the paintings and became transfixed by it. There were eyes in the painting that seemed to follow her, so she walked around the room again, idly glancing at the other three paintings.

Suddenly, she felt strangely trapped and claustrophobic, so much so, she moved back to the bench, where she picked up some of her things to go, including her bag. A noise in the room distracted her; it was a bit like leaves being trodden on. Turning and looking at the painting where the sound came from, she noticed everything seemed to be moving. There were green eyes in a turquoise sky. Spinning around the eyes, there were autumn leaves, and they were falling to the ground, where a man was walking away. As he did so, he trod on the dead dry leaves.

At the side of the painting was a card saying,
Title: UOY.
Not for sale. Do not touch the paintings.

The woman opened her handbag to take out her spectacles. In some ways, they made her look even more attractive. She placed them on her beautiful nose and brushed her long auburn hair. She felt the need to touch the falling leaves. Despite the sign saying do not touch the paintings, she did.

A short time later, the owner of the gallery went round checking the rooms, something she often did. In the white walls room, on the white bench, she found a paper coffee cup, a paper bag with a half-eaten sandwich, a banana skin and a small black jacket. She picked up the things and walked back to reception, and said to the receptionist,
"More for the lost property cupboard."

2 The homeless man.

It had been a bitter night. The cold wind had chilled his very core. Usually, he was able to find a place, out of the direct winter wind, but last night he was moved on by the police. If it wasn't for his dog, who knows if he would have made it through the night?

It was early morning. He wanted the time to go quicker, because he knew a place nearby where he could warm his bones. If he was quick and quiet, he could catch up on some lost sleep.

At nine-thirty, he gathered his frugal belongings, which he stuffed into an old camouflage bag, along with a few bits of cardboard which remained poking out of the top. He stood up and then swung the bag over his shoulder. A pale blue sky and a watery sun silhouetted the concrete skyline. He grimaced with his aches and pains, then moved on from the shop doorway. He caught his reflection in the glass. He had a scarf tucked several times around his head, a long unshaven beard and he was wearing an old moth-eaten coat. He seemed to be in his late forties; washed and shaved he would probably look a lot younger. Close by his side, there was a 57 varieties medium-sized dog which had turned up one night out of the blue. Since then, he had stuck with the man, even though he had been told to go away.

He walked about half a mile, past other doorways with more homeless people encamped outside, until he came to some white marble steps, where he sat for a while. He had been here before. He took out an old cap from an inside pocket and placed it on the floor. The odd passer-by dropped a few pence into it, some spoke to his dog, but no-one spoke to him. It wasn't long before he had enough cash to buy a coffee.

At ten o'clock, he walked a few hundred yards through the streets of the city, now a hive of activity, to a popular back street.

The large, impressive glass frontage of the gallery allowed him to see the receptionist, who was busying herself. The man knew from past experience that she left the reception area at this time every day. He also knew she opened the door before she did this. This was his opportunity to go into the gallery, unnoticed, like he had done before.

Like clockwork, the receptionist did her job. He slipped in, passed the reception area, then went towards the main gallery, but, hearing someone coming, he turned into the white walls room, where he had been before. The gallery, on the whole, was quiet in the morning, so he knew he could get some sleep in a warm corner somewhere. He walked round the room, dog in tow, settling for the far corner where he and the dog could snuggle up warm.

He awoke shortly afterwards from a strange dream, rubbed his eyes and looked up at the paintings. He got up and walked around the room. He stared at one of the paintings. He didn't like it, it reminded him of something he wanted to forget.

Immediately, his cold, tired mind placed him in his own house, many years ago, with his own things around him. He felt the room, the time, the place. He saw his wife dead on the floor, her body in a pool of blood. In a fit of jealousy, he had killed her, because she was having an affair. He had followed her to a hotel where he saw her with another man.

He confronted her when she got home. Losing his temper, it was over so quickly, but he then spent many hours not knowing what to do.

Some time later, as he got to grips with himself, he decided to dispose of the body. When it got dark, he dug a hole in the back garden, dragged her body out, wrapped in black plastic bags and buried her.

He tried to carry on, pretending that she had gone to her mother's, but eventually, friends and relatives became suspicious.

Then, one night, he left, leaving everything behind, with just £500 in cash.

That was ten years ago. He still feared the madness (having been close to killing others over the years, usually when he had got drunk on cheap booze), but he always held back because of the past.

As he looked at the painting, he saw a foot, a leg, a hand and other parts of a body, strangely placed as if they were in a garden. He felt sick. He sat down anxiously, opposite the painting, noticing that the dog was still asleep. He got up and walked over to the painting. He looked at the words at the side of the painting.

Title: TES.
Not for sale. Do not touch the paintings.

In the painting he could still see the body parts, but now it was as if they were moving.
The man looked down to see and hear his dog, who was now crying and pawing at his feet.
"It's ok," he said to the dog. "But this is strange."
The man looked even closer at the painting, finding it unbelievably relaxing. He moved his hand to touch it.

Later that day, the homeless man's old, grubby camouflage knapsack, with bits of cardboard sticking out of the top, were found on the floor in the gallery. It was not saved in the lost property cupboard but thrown unceremoniously into the bin.

3 The Priest

He was prostrate before the altar, his head full of the sound of prayers and confession. Easing himself up with his solid gold-top walking stick, he crossed himself and kissed his rosary.

The years of praying, being a priest, were second nature to him. His faith was like the blood that ran through him. He was unshakable.
The church doors creaked and whined as they opened, then footsteps found their way to the pews. The parishioners would take a seat and make their peace with God. The priest, as mediator and translator of God's law, would then absolve them of their sins. He looked up at the great stained-glass window. Christ was up there on the cross, the sun highlighting all the colours of the rainbow, framed by a great arch in the window.
Today, he walked past the waiting few and made his way

through the church, his cane tapping out the clear sound. As he left the sound dissipated.

He was a small man with greying hair and skin, a stoop that had become his demeanour over many years in prayer, but today his eyes looked as if all hope had gone. Dressed in black and with an even darker mind, the lines on his face were a highway of bad thoughts and feelings.

A short walk from his church led the priest to the doors of the gallery. Opening the door to the large glass reception-area, he nodded to the receptionist, who returned his nod. He would come here often, for his own absolution. He'd walk slowly around the gallery, until he could find a painting that inspired him, then he would sit and pray.

Today he was drawn to the white walls room, where he felt immediately at peace as he entered. Drawn to one painting, he immediately went down on his knees, with the aid of his gold-top stick, and started to pray.

The priest had, at one time, been so much taller, but the years had worn him down, not just dealing with other people's sins, but also his own, which had withered his mind.

This particular morning, he had received a letter in the post and also a phone call from the bishop, asking him to answer questions about his relationships with the children; those who had sung in the church choir, when he first arrived at his church, over forty years ago.

When the priest was younger, he had been long in step, strong of mind, and he also had a good voice. He would lead the choir, which in itself led to things he would rather not think about, concerning some of the boys in the choir.

In light of people investigating the church and its past misdemeanours, now *his* misdemeanour, it was his own sin which was now in the spotlight.

21

The prayer was audible, with the priest rocking back and forth, as if in some way it might find its way to God more quickly. No-one was around. It was as if this was his own church, his direct line to the heavens. Suddenly hearing something, he opened one eye, then the other one, slowly. Looking up at the painting, he thought he saw the moon that was high in a dark foreboding sky. The light from the moon then caught the shape of a body kneeling. He got up to take a closer look. He seemed hypnotised by the moon's radiating light, as it bathed the praying figure.

"A sign," he thought, "if ever there was one."

At the side of the painting it said,

Title: EM
Not for sale. Do not touch the painting.

He saw the shining moon as a message from God. Tears began to fall from his eyes, as he lifted his finger to touch the penitent figure in the painting.

A solid gold-topped walking stick lay on the floor of the gallery. It was found later and left in lost property.

4 The bully

He stood before the other directors and ordered them to back him, which they did, but only because if they didn't, the company would surely fold. He was used to getting his own way, he always had.

Caterers had set up the function room in the gallery, in expectation of at least a hundred people. It was in honour of his leadership over the years. He was sixty. He was not ready for retirement, but he knew it wouldn't be long. His wife sat loyally by him. She was tiny in comparison to this big man. She was a small shadow. He had tried to keep fit over the years, but had put weight on, making his wife look even smaller by comparison. His board members still believed in him. His wife didn't.

Over the years, his wife had always been there to back him, but at a price. They had two children, both grown up and gone, happier to be thousands of miles away, rather than where their bully father was.

Their mother encouraged them to go, even though he wanted them to join the company and carry on the company name. Years ago, when they were small, they'd hear their father shouting at their mother. The children would stay huddled together in their bedroom till the next day, when they would find their mother, who would be covered in bruises. Years went by, the bruises became fewer because he hit her where it couldn't be seen. As the children grew, they hated their father more and encouraged their mother to go to the police. She never did. When they were old enough, the children left home. Both found work and homes abroad.

This woman thought it was her duty to serve this man, but she hated him, hated him so much, yet knew of no way to stop this horrible torture. Her children constantly asked her to leave him and go abroad and live with them, but she always said no.

He stood up to make his speech. It was barnstorming stuff, but he overplayed it. As he sat down, he said to his wife,
"I feel ill, take me home."
Dutifully, his wife helped him out of the room and through the gallery.
"I need help!" she said. "You're heavy!"
"For fuck's sake woman, get me out of here!"
She managed to get to the lower corridor, where he said,
"I think I feel a bit better. The pain is easing. Let me sit down."
She saw the white bench in the white walls room, so she let him sit in there. He breathed more easily.
"Wait here," she said, "I'll get the chauffeur to take us home."
She left the room.

As the big man sat, he took off his tie and his jacket, then looked up at the painting in front of him. He saw a yellow sun shining down on a cemetery, with one headstone standing out from the others. He wasn't sure, but he could have sworn that the grave seemed to open. Was it the light, the shadows or was he a bit drunk?

He smiled to himself, saying,

"What awful shit!"

At the side of the painting it said,

Title: EERF

Not for sale. Do not touch the painting.

In a fit of rage, he ripped the painting off the wall, and threw it on the floor.

Ten minutes later, his wife came back with the chauffeur to the gallery, where they found just her husband's tie and jacket on the white bench and a painting lying on the floor. They both looked around the gallery, not sure where her husband could be, then his wife decided to go home, thinking that he may have gone home by taxi. The receptionist of the gallery said, "I can't remember seeing him leave, but it's been very busy tonight." His wife was also confused as to why he had left his coat and tie behind. As she was leaving, she picked up the painting and placed it back on the wall.

That night after everyone had gone, in the darkness of the gallery, security lights glowed here and there. The reception area was still bathed in light.

5 The white walls room

In the white walls room, the four paintings seemed to have a life of their own, with movement in each one and colours of every kind. The spotlights above each painting went on and off, in time to the beating of a heart. The air was humid, almost like water that had been poured on hot stones. A mist seemed to rise from the paintings and settle like a fog in the room. It was still and silent, then the sound of someone breathing deeply, followed by quiet groaning was heard. A shape of sorts was appearing on the white bench in the centre of the room.

As the fog settled, there was what seemed to be a figure, difficult to discern as it moved, because it was dressed in an assortment of garb.

It attempted to stand and as it did so, an old scarf hung over its shoulders and around its head. It was also wearing black trousers with diagonal red streaks cutting through them and a long brown coat, dotted with white shapes. For all the world, it looked like a human clothes horse.

The figure gathered itself, stretched its fingers and arms, rolled its head from side to side, looked at its hands and down at its feet.

It stepped carefully down off the white bench and turned towards the door, then walked in the direction of the reception area, as if it knew where to go. It moved with a slight limp. As it reached the back of the reception area, it opened a cupboard door at the back, inside of which the lost property was kept. In there, it found a walking stick with a solid gold top. It pulled the stick out. As it walked towards the reception doors, a sigh of relief could be faintly heard.

It pressed the security door-release button, causing the intruder alarm to go off but, within a few seconds, the figure had left the building, being followed closely by a medium-sized dog.

6 The detective

The next morning, a detective accompanied by his assistant called at the reception of the gallery. He showed the receptionist his warrant card. The receptionist called the owner of the gallery; the detective and his assistant went to interview her in the white walls room. The forensics team had already been. The owner of the gallery was sitting looking at one of the paintings on the wall as the detective came in. The owner shook the detective's hand, then asked him to sit on the white bench. He looked at the painting, then looked at her.

She said, with a sound of shock in her voice,

"It's gone! They've all gone!"

"What do you mean, they've gone?" asked the detective. She composed herself and said,

"The canvases are still there but the paintings which were on them have gone."

The detective got up and walked around the room. All the canvases were blank.

"How do you know they are the same canvases?" he said.

"On the back of each painting there is a signature and an authenticity label," she said.

The detective asked,

"Have you reviewed your CCTV?"

She replied, "My staff are doing it now."

Together, they went to the control room to see.

In a separate room behind reception, they went through the last 24 hours CCTV. They saw the businessman and his wife go into the room.

The detective said,

"Hang on a moment! Is there a camera in the room?"

The owner said,

"No, just outside the opening. We didn't think it necessary. Anyway, it was a new room, especially for this exhibition. We wanted to create a room of peace."

At that moment, the detective received a phone call, following which he informed the owner,

"The businessman's wife reported her husband missing this morning."

They continued looking through more of the CCTV, noticing that the businessman never left the room. The detective then asked,

"How often do you go through your CCTV?"

"Rarely. If nothing happens, why would we?" she answered.

The detective said,

"Can we go back over the last week on your CCTV?"

They made themselves comfortable, then established that, over the last week on consecutive days, three other people and a dog went into the white walls room and never came out.

The feeling of shock and disbelief was tangible as they watched it over and over again. This was now more than just the disappearance of paint on canvases. It was now about four missing persons and a dog.

They moved the recording forward to the last moments on the CCTV, and the figure that set the alarms off, watching it as it moved towards reception. They saw it lean into the lost-property cupboard and retrieve a gold-topped walking stick. They could only see the shadowed figure, its shape and demeanour, because the clothes and scarf allowed no clear shot of its face. So, there was no knowing as to what sex it was. All they could see was that the person was being followed by a medium-sized dog.

As with all things, time goes by. No leads were found on the missing persons, not even the dog. A search was set up for the figure who had left the gallery that morning, but apart from a few items of clothing found in the general direction it had gone, no more information was uncovered. The clothes were tested for DNA, but no match was found.

7 The prisoner

For many years, the prisoner painted in his cell. He was famous, a famous serial-killer. When he was tried and sentenced, they said he would rot in prison; words which haunted him, having always said he was innocent.

Many, many times, he asked his lawyers to investigate new evidence, but nothing was found to help him. He remained in jail until his death.

While in prison he kept himself to himself, so he spent all his time learning. He studied the great master painters and their ability to use the paint to lure the viewer in, to hypnotise, to seduce and beguile. He studied the mixing of paint and alchemy, so he could draw people towards a piece of his artwork. He would ask for books from reference libraries and use what he found, then weave a spell on whoever might be pulled towards his paintings.

On the day of his death, he lay with his paintings in his cell, along with those he had bequeathed to relatives and a friend. He asked that four in particular should never be sold, but only that they should be shown in galleries in a certain way. Of course, this was agreed, because everyone thought that his paintings would just be stored somewhere forever and forgotten about.

Months after he died, a friend of the painter killed himself. He owned up to being the serial killer and left a letter saying that the painter was innocent, and that he had planted evidence to say the painter was guilty. In his suicide note, he'd written, "I cannot live! My mind seems to be melting. The painter who was sent to prison is innocent."

At the scene of his suicide, they found a bucket of water with blood in it, nothing else.

Sitting against a wall in his apartment was a painting that had been left to him by his friend, the painter. It was an abstract painting of a bucket with a single dead flower in it and a drop of blood running down the side into the water.

8 UOY TES EM EERF

In time to come, the Gallery was the most visited exhibition since records began. The four paintings, still clearly blank, being linked to the story, caught the imagination of everyone who visited. The four paintings are still not for sale.

YOU SET ME FREE.

BRUCE AND JULIA

The sun was shining brightly through the window onto the apartment wall. As it crept across, it caught a large mirror that was hanging there, then reflected across the room, where it shone directly on Julia, who was half-awake in bed.

Julia pulled the duvet up over her head and groaned. Almost immediately, she felt something thud onto her now covered-up head. Her eyes rolled as she knew what it was - her cat Bruce. Bruce thought this was the time to play, as Julia often got Bruce onto the bed, covered her up and played games with her. Yes, her - Bruce the cat was a female. Julia had once had an Australian boyfriend called Bruce. When he unceremoniously dumped Julia, she felt low. So much so, she adopted an abandoned cat to replace him. It wasn't till later that she found out the cat was a girl, but the name stuck.

Unfortunately, Julia was not in the mood for all this. She was at home because she felt ill. In truth, she was looking for a new job, a new life, a new something. Bruce seemed to sympathise. There was another thud. This time, Bruce jumped off the duvet onto the floor and ran out of the room, her tail in the air, as if it was her decision to stop playing, which of course it was.

Bruce was now in the other room, doing what cats do after they have had something to eat. You could see on Bruce's face it was a nearly perfect start to the day; eat, play (well nearly), use the litter tray, lick every nook and cranny till it was clean. From her bedroom, Julia shrieked,

"Is that you Bruce? That stinks worse than a man."

Bruce, for one moment, stopped mid-lick, gave what looked like a smile, then carried on regardless. Julia got up. She lived in a two-room apartment, one big room for living, eating, entertaining friends, watching tv and slouching on the old sofa - this was her best and favourite thing to do. Then there was the bedroom, with a curtained-off shower and toilet in the corner, which Julia loved. When she was on her own, the curtain just stayed open; the ease of it, from toilet to bed, in a few steps, and vice-versa.

Bruce also liked the curtain. He would climb to the top sometimes, when Julia was in the shower, then he'd jump down and frighten the hell out of Julia.

At that moment in time, men didn't seem to fit into Julia's life. She would call the relationships "flings", which seemed to last long enough for the man to say, "Let's move in together!" That was when Julia ended it.

Bruce, having finished her daily clean, was now walking with a swagger, like, "Look at me, I'm the cat's pyjamas!"

Bruce was feeling good. Julia was feeling shit.

She made some coffee. For a change, she had a caramel latte. "Why the fuck is it called latte? It's milky shit coffee!" she shouted.

Bruce was on the counter work-top, very prim, very proper, looking at Julia with disdain.

"Ok, Bruce, apart from stinking out my flat, what have you been doing? I suppose you were out last night with the men cats, selling yourself short with that ginger tom from the basement flat."

Bruce looked the other way. She knew when Julie was on the warpath, so it was best to give her room until she got it out of her system. This was no hormonal thing. At that present moment, it was a war zone.

Bruce jumped onto the floor and made her way into the bedroom. Julia watched and wished that her own life was that simple. Once in the bedroom, Bruce curled up in the dishevelled duvet. There was nothing better than sleeping in Julia's duvet; it was so human.

Julia drank her milky coffee, which seemed to ease her tension. She ate some toast, leaving the crust. She was at her kitchen table with her laptop open, making her way through her emails. Ninety-nine per cent was junk, the other one per cent was old emails. She scrolled through and closed the page. She googled this and that, but she lost interest, got up and looked out of her window. There was a small balcony with a single door to the side of the window. She opened it, stood on the balcony, where there was no room for a chair or a table; a pot-plant would fill the space up. It was pretty useless normally, but today it was useful.

It was the middle of May. A warm morning breeze caught Julia's long, soft, highlighted hair, which, when loose, came down to her waist with a natural soft curl. Most the of time she tied it back. She was a young, old-fashioned hippie. There was the odd tattoo here and there and, of course, earrings, the more extravagant the better. She was a part-time veggie-cum-vegan. Part-time because she wasn't sure. Sometimes she would crave bacon, cook it, eat it, then regret it.

The human condition doesn't always leave room for scruples. She wasn't tall, but she wasn't small either. Her friends would say she was cute like Kylie Minogue (who Julia hated), some would say she was just right, others would say she was a pain in the arse.

Today she was angry. She took in the cacophony of the city, the smell and outright pollution. She breathed it into her lungs and mind, then screamed, as loud as anyone could, four floors up in an apartment block. She looked down at the people moving along the roads and footpaths. Hardly anyone looked up; those who did, carried on their way, regardless.

Bruce heard the scream, but she wasn't bothered. She knew Julia, her ways and her moods. She also heard the door slam, then Julia's gentle weeping. Bruce got back to her own thoughts and started to dream about how she first met the handsome Siamese cat.

Bruce had a crush on a sleek Siamese cat that lived in the penthouse suite, two blocks along and up. She therefore spent very little time in the alley. Well, now and again, she would find herself there, but ginger toms didn't really do it for her.

It wasn't easy falling for a posh cat. For a start, they are never let out, so no chance of a bit of romance, without some really hard work.

Julia's flat had a cat-flap, so Bruce came and went as she pleased. Sometimes it was difficult but, most of the time, there was a window left slightly open on the landing, which had three doors to other apartments, as well as a lift. Bruce would occasionally slip into the lift, if one of the neighbours was using it, but, most of the time, the window was open. There was a tricky jump to a lower roof, but she was well-versed in how to achieve it without too much trouble, even though it was many floors up. When on the roof, Bruce slipped easily from one roof to another, the last bit being trickier.

The penthouse apartment was almost like a castle, to forestall all invasions, just in case there was a war, or peasants or just anyone who would want to invade. For Bruce, it was a challenge. She had found a balcony that wrapped around the lower apartments. These being more expensive than Julia's, they linked flat to flat with a small divider. Most had chairs and tables or plant pots, a few had sun-loungers. Bruce eased her way around the edge of the apartments, taking her time. Sometimes people were on their balconies, so she had to be careful then. Some residents were mean and would shout at her and shoo her away, others would fuss her, even giving her titbits. Eventually, Bruce would negotiate the balcony and then, at the end, she would jump onto a sloping roof opposite the penthouse. A few jumps later, she would find herself high up above all the other buildings, ready for one last jump to her destination.

She was there, on a low wall that surrounded a beautiful patio area, which had a pond containing fish, a fountain and many plant pots. It was stunningly beautiful, but it was all lost on Bruce. She was just a curious cat. Somehow the space brought out her femininity. She seemed to sway like a model on a catwalk. Then she got closer to a block of glass doors that wrapped around the centre of the roof space. She caught her reflection in the dark smoked glass. Now she could see how beautiful she was. She got closer and tried to see inside.

"Bruce! Bruce!"

Bruce slowly opened her eyes and saw Julia beaming at her. "Were you dreaming about the ginger tom? You looked as if you were running around in your dream, making a din as well!" Bruce looked insulted, sat up and started to lick her paws. "Come on! No more of that nonsense! Off the duvet, it's time for the wash!"

Everything ended up on the floor. This would have been the perfect time for Bruce to join in have fun, but not today. She was beside herself with indignation. Ginger Tom indeed! She slunk off to the kitchen.

Julia was feeling marginally better, so time to put bad thoughts to one side, hence the cleaning. The washing machine was working hard; Julia had gone into overdrive.

Bruce had taken up a spot on a sunny windowsill, watching Julia from a distance, as well as all this mad activity. She settled down to dream again about the handsome Siamese cat. Finding herself back outside the glass doors, she continued to stare into the window, which was difficult, because not only was there a tint to them, but also the sun was shining right across the patio. Bruce turned to go, then, out of the corner of her eye spotted movement on the other side of the glass. A sleek figure was coming towards her. Bruce could see a beautifully handsome Siamese cat sitting down on the other side of the glass. He looked royal, he looked sublime. Further round the other side of the patio, a door slid open. Nine out of ten cats would now ske-daddle, but Bruce was in love. The Siamese cat seemed to smile, which melted Bruce's heart.

At that moment, a size ten shoe hit her squarely on her back, as she heard a screaming voice shout,

"Gitoutofit!"

She didn't need an invitation! Bruce was gone. She flew over the roofs, full of that hideous feeling of embarrassment, desperate to escape the screeching sound.

She had awoken from the dream, which was in fact a reality and she could still feel the pain of that shoe.

Julia had settled down to her day. She was now feeling fine with only a small nagging feeling in her stomach. She was a freelance technician, excellent with computers, who had built up a repu-tation, having knowledge of things dark. If you had a virus, she'd fix it, one way or another. The thing was, she was stuck with the same companies, two high-street names, who paid well, regu-larly. She was safe, but not happy; she wanted more edge.

She had emailed the companies, saying she felt unwell and needed a few weeks off. Of course, they complained a little, but not too much. She was that good, each of the companies had offered her a full-time job not long ago. She had turned them both down.

Bruce had woken up. Even though she kept getting that recur-ring dream and could still feel the bruises, she wanted so much to go back, to see the Siamese.

The tv was on. Julia was flicking channels. She hardly ever watched tv, usually her iPad or iPhone would dominate her evening, but she had switched them off. She had had a shower and was in a rabbit onesie, with her feet up, eating a bowl of crisps. Bruce sauntered over, not sure of the reception she might get. Julia looked across at her and smiled. Bruce started purring before she got to Julia, then just rolled onto her lap.

The next day, Bruce woke up on the sofa, felt no real urge in any of the necessary areas, so went back to sleep. Meanwhile, Julia, however, was wide awake, showered and ready to go. Bruce could hear her singing; this was different. Bruce leapt up onto the countertop to watch.

The radio was on loud and Julia was wacky-dancing; no real rhythm, just shaking it about. Bruce walked along the top of the counter, as Julia mimed, then sang loudly along to Dancing Queen, before picking up Bruce and twirling her round and round in her arms. Having been placed back on the counter, Bruce groggily weaved across it, nearly falling off the edge of the countertop, much to the merriment of Julia.

Julia drank her coffee, then had a banana and an orange. Bruce licked her paws. She knew Julia was now on another health kick.

"Hey Bruce! Just had a call from a contact! It seems that the people in the penthouse suite, two blocks down and up, need my expertise! Might be a good call and it's only five minutes away."

It wasn't long before Julia was putting on her coat and getting ready to leave. Bruce was weaving in and out of her legs, so she picked her up and started talking childlike.

"It's ok puddykins! I'll be back soon!"

Then she continued to kiss Bruce, placed her on the floor and waved, as she went through the door, like a breath of fresh air.

Bruce was lost. For one moment, she felt almost human. She wanted Julia to walk back through the door and dance with her again. Ten minutes later, after a large plate of Cattybiccies, followed by the use of the litter tray, Bruce was licking herself from head to foot, when she caught a reflection of herself in a mirror and thought how beautiful she was, black and sleek, with white tips to her ears and tail. She stood, did a sort of turn to make sure she looked good all round; there was no question of that. Things to do and now was the time to move.

Bruce slipped effortlessly through the cat flap, then made the short leap to the nearest roof from the open window on the landing. The sun was bouncing off the roof tiles. They were warm and Bruce was in the mood for love.

Julia looked good in her new jeans, red shoes, short denim jacket and pink shirt, her hair tied up with multicoloured beads which cascaded down around her neck and shoulders. She walked as if she was happy; quick, defined steps with Dancing Queen in her head. What a difference a day off can do!

Julia had been given a security PIN number to use, in order to enter the apartment building. The entrance hall was twice the size of her flat. There were plant pots with tall palms and floor-to-ceiling glass mirrors, which made it look even bigger. On the opposite side of the hall, there was a board with a list of residents in gold letters. In one of the glass walls, there were two fire doors. Above one, it said "Apartments", above the other, "Penthouse Suite".

Julia went through the penthouse suite door, noticing, to the side of the lift, a telephone. She picked it up. A voice said, "Yes?" She said her name. Immediately, the lift showed a green light and the doors opened. The strange thing was, inside the lift, there was another palm. Julia thought this was funny - a plant that was always on the move. On the lift wall it said Penthouse Suite, which Julia found equally funny, because it was too small to be one.

Julia immediately noticed the background music, slightly Asian in style and quite catchy. She felt an urge to move her body to the sound, but, just as she was mid-movement, the lift doors opened. Standing opposite her was a man with a quizzical look on his face. Lowering her hands to her side, she smiled. He half-smiled back. The Asian guy was about five foot tall, dressed in black t-shirt and trousers, with bare feet. She felt sure he was shorter than her. He stared at her without expression. Then he looked down at her feet; she did too.

As she stepped out of the lift, Julia took off her shoes. Now she was the same size as him. She was guessing he was not the owner of the penthouse. He gave a her a bigger smile, then gestured and said,

"Follow me!"

She did so. She bit her lip. So far, the whole thing had amused her, following the Asian guy. He seemed to sway his hips, almost like a galleon at sea. She soon snapped out of it, struck dumb by the size of the place. Her flat would be lost in the hall area alone. There were works of art on each wall, so tastefully exhibited. At the end of the hall, he opened the door and ushered Julia in.

This room was small in comparison, with a glass wall all around it. Strangely, the glass was changing colours, making it very relaxing, but this felt like an office, rather than a home. Still, she was amazed. The room was minimal: two formal chairs and a large glass desk. A guy was sat behind it. He said,

"Hello, I'm Theo Able."

He stood up, walked around the desk, shook Julia's hand, and said,

"Julia, you come highly recommended."

Theo was tall, though not too tall. After all, most people were tall compared to Julia. He was dressed stylishly but informally in a cream shirt with black trousers, both creaseless. His hair, complexion and chiselled good looks made her think of a Italian Casanova. She was now feeling a bit out of her depth and, what's more, attracted to this guy. Never one to mix with customers, her role normally being through a third party, she felt awkward.

She sat opposite Theo Able. He made her aware that he needed to sketch in his background. As she would be looking at his computers, it was important to have her understand his business. She tried not to let her mouth drop open, as he talked about his mini empire, his import-export business, works of art and antiques. All the time he was speaking, she felt in a dreamlike state, as his words seemed to undress her. She snapped out of it when he stopped talking and thought about the job in hand. Whilst one side of her mind was trying to digest all this information, another part was saying,

"Are you talking to me or someone else?"

However, one thing he said at the end of their chat stuck in her head - his passion for Siamese cats, how he bred them and idolised them, adding that his own prized possession was indeed a Siamese cat, which was perfect in every way and lived there in the penthouse.

"Maybe," he added, "you would like to meet him later?"

For a second, it almost felt like she was going to be introduced to royalty. She was flattered, yet also amused.

Theo stood up. Julia automatically did the same.

"Before any more business, I would like to show you around," he said, pressing a button on the desk. All the doors folded back, revealing a palatial space, mainly on three split floors. It looked almost like a spaceship! As they walked and looked around, she could see several floors with different sets of stairs going up and down.

She thought it was awesome; not a word she liked, but it suited here perfectly. Thick pile carpet covered every floor whilst the walls displayed yet more paintings and works of art.

Each wall contained glass with changing patterns, all of which subdued the atmosphere. Pieces of furniture were few and far between, but each one was superbly tasteful.

Theo walked her around, talking to her. She was already washed away.

"As you can see," he said, "security is very important to me."

Julia looked at him and stared. She was trying to speak, but the words were somewhere else. A few moments passed. She snapped out of it. She wanted this job so badly and didn't want to seem like an ignoramus. The words finally came, but not the ones she wanted.

"Why don't you live in the country? You could have a mansion in the sticks."

He smiled, then replied,

"Yes, but I need the city. Everything is here. Anyway, my place in the country is a place of leisure, not business."

Julia decided she should not speak unless she knew what she was saying. He looked at her, knowing how intimidating this must be.

"I do my own checks on everyone I deal with."

Giving her a calm smile, he continued,

"I only work with those I feel I can trust."

She coloured up and felt like he could see her underwear.

Yet she didn't feel unnerved, because she knew she would do the same, but maybe not try to see his underwear.

He took her up the stairs to the roof area. This was more intimate, not a wide-open space, just enough room for a big sofa, a coffee table, a very large modern bookcase full of hundreds of books and yet more large palms situated by the doors.

At the touch of another button, doors opened all the way round onto a beautiful sunny day. The space was wonderful, with more small palm trees gently moving in the warm wind. They walked around the patio area. Julia was shell-shocked by it all, only managing to say,

"Wow! Amazing! Fantastic!" before biting her lip because she felt like a child in a sweet shop. She was so impressed by it all. Then, suddenly, out of the corner of her eye, she saw Bruce. She was skirting the wall, making her way towards the open doors. Julia thought for a second.

"Erm, do you have CCTV up here?"

"No, not on the roof," he replied. "The chances of anyone getting up here are remote and, even if they did, they couldn't get through the doors."

He then pointed at the metal shutters that came discreetly down, outside the glass. Julia, who was now facing Theo, with her hands behind her back, gestured to Bruce not to go through the doors. Bruce, of course, ignored her.

Julia immediately said,

"Shit!"

"Pardon?"

"Sorry!" she continued, "I'm so overcome by this place! It's just an expression."

"It's strange actually," said Theo, as he went to move away, "no-one could get up here, but my manservant saw a black cat on this roof space, only the other day. He had to chase it away. Well, he threw something at it, so I don't think it will be back. I should get CCTV on here. I don't want any other cats near my Siamese."

"Yes! Good idea!" agreed Julia calmly, whilst thinking that Bruce was loose inside his beautiful apartment and there was fuck-all she could do!

With the doors closed, they went back to the table where they had been earlier. Theo's systems were all set into the glass table. Now Julia was even more impressed. He logged himself in and told her about the glitches that had not been fixed by the makers of the computer programmes. This was where Julia was at her best. Theo said,

"I trust you can solve the problem, as I would like to leave you for a moment to make an important call."

Julia was well-aware she had a problem with her bloody cat, but a lucrative job was in the balance. She familiarised herself with the system.

Bruce, herself, was on a different mission, to find her love, without a single thought of any trouble she might be causing. She was doing what cats do, going from room to room, not the slightest bit impressed by the thickness of the carpet or the paintings on the wall. She was in love. She made her way through the bedrooms and anterooms, around the edge of the penthouse suite. She came to a door, slightly ajar, and sneaked in. She could smell him. He was in that room. Bruce miaowed affectionately, the Siamese opened one eye, then the other, as he nestled in his master's duvet.

Julia was now well into Theo's computer system. With half her mind on the damn cat, she easily sorted the glitches, then also noticed the CCTV system and reviewed it. She saw herself enter the apartments, the lift and the hall, noticed that the Asian guy had gone out, then spotted Bruce sauntering through the hall, past the lift and into another room.

"Shit!" Julia thought, "That fucking cat!"

Within minutes, Theo was back. Julia explained her modifications, adding that it would wise to use a second security programme to help, all the time. Whilst doing so, she was thinking,

"What the hell's my cat doing?"
Theo asked,
"You like coffee? I'm afraid my manservant is out, so I'll make it."
"Yes please," she replied.
Theo pressed another button further into the apartment, allowing more doors to magically open. He looked at Julia. "Now you can see why the computer must run smoothly."

After asking how she liked her coffee, he walked down some stairs. Julia could see a kitchen area - it was like the Star Ship Enterprise.
A few minutes later, she could hear a strange meowing that grated her ears. It lasted several minutes. Julia could see that Theo was on the phone again. She immediately found the controls on the computer for the music that was in the background, then turned it up to cover the noise. She saw Theo look towards her. She mouthed "Just testing!" as the meowing eased down.
Julia viewed the CCTV again, saw Bruce running through the hall and knew straight away that she was looking for an escape route, so Julia pressed the button to the roof doors. Heading straight towards them, Bruce ran past Julia, who immediately closed them quickly, when she could see on the CCTV that Bruce was clear.
Theo came walking up the stairs with the coffee. Julia erased the CCTV footage containing Bruce. As Theo put the coffee onto the table, he asked,
"Did you hear some high-pitched noises?"
Julia replied,
"Yes! I think it was reverb on your speaker system. I retuned it."
Ten minutes later, with coffee and checking all finished, Theo guided her to the lift and said,
"Thank you. I'll be in touch."
Julia's heart was beating fifteen to the dozen. She was just glad to be out of there. Under her breath, she muttered,
"Fucking cat!"

Then she thought about the royal Siamese cat that Theo owned that she had never managed to see. She wasn't disappointed, just relieved.

By the time she was on the street, she needed a drink, so she met up with a friend from work, a guy she had been out with a couple of times. Nothing serious, but she liked him.

She walked into the bar they had agreed to meet at. Danny was sitting at a high table, with a drink in his hand. He also had a bottle of wine and two glasses. Julia sat down. Danny poured the wine. She downed hers in one.

"Wow-a! What's the hurry?"

Julia explained, "I got a job! Well, I did some freelance work. Not sure I've got anything, but still, I'm feeling great!"

Danny smiled and they shared another glass of wine. He wasn't bad-looking. He was at least six inches taller than Julia, with a short Peaky Blinders haircut, sharp features, but warm, loving eyes. At that moment in time, it was all that Julia needed.

Julia had her arm high over Danny's shoulder, as they both fell into the hallway of her apartment building. They helped each other walk up the stairs as the lift was out of order and, after much laughing and falling down, they got to her apartment. The key was difficult to get in the hole, but they managed it and crashed into her place and onto the sofa.

Bruce was on the windowsill, looking pleased with herself but disapproving of this behaviour, as Julia and Danny were laid on the settee, Danny half across Julia, legs akimbo. Julia's eyes opened slightly, enough to catch Bruce's eye.

"And you, you dirty little madam, what the hell were you doing? You might have ruined the best chance of work ever!"

Bruce looked crest-fallen. Julia untangled herself from Danny, then swayed across the room and prodded Bruce in the side of her furry black coat. She wagged her finger. Danny woke. He said, "What's up? What's the matter?" Julia continued.

"I'll tell you what's the matter! My cat Bruce here has been shmoosing with some posh Siamese cat at my client's apartment!"

Danny stood up and weaved towards Julia. They both started to lecture the cat.

Bruce had had enough.

Julia she could cope with, but not Danny. No! She jumped down off the windowsill and went into the bedroom.

Julia slurred,

"Go on you little hussie!"

At which point, Julia crashed out onto the sofa. Danny followed with a little less finesse. They lay there in a communal mound, burping and farting. Not a pretty sight or sound.

The next morning, the flat was quiet, apart from shallow snores. When Julia woke, she noticed an awful smell, as she lay prostrate across the settee with her eyes closed, she said. "For God's sake, Bruce! Is that you again?"

She opened her eyes to see Bruce sitting on her chest, purring happily, then she heard Danny's voice,

"I'm sorry about that! I had to go!"

"Use the spray, that's what it's there for!" shouted Julia.

A few months passed by. Things were much the same yet different. Julia's job absorbed more of her time, but she was happy for it. Theo, her new client, had lots of friends. Julia got more lucrative contacts. Danny moved in.

And Bruce? Bruce was found one morning under Julia's bed, giving birth to three beautiful Siamese-ish kittens and, believe it or not, one ginger one. Bruce must have been spreading her bets.....

Oh, and Danny built a dividing-wall and door between the bedroom and the bathroom.

PS. They kept the ginger Tom.

FIVE GHOSTS

When we dream, is it possible that ghosts come to inhabit our thoughts, to regale themselves inside our heads? Then plunder, excite, tease and test us? In waking, are we beguiled by the meaning in the stew that's left behind, or are they just trying to right the wrongs, to straighten out the good, the bad and the lost among us? It seems to me that ghosts have no gender, colour, race, religion, let alone biological specification and, whether you believe or not, they are here.

Ghost 1

Jan was walking slowly down a windswept street, the house lights, as well as the streetlights, a blur. It was early evening in mid-November. It was dark, the rain almost nailing her to the pavement, but she ignored it. Her step was steady and slow, her mind darker than the night, colder than a block of ice.
Jan kept her pace, her mind elsewhere. Her body was like a metronome, her feet hitting the floor with an audible splash. It seemed that nothing would shift her off course.

Jan was almost there. She looked up, as the station got closer. The orange glow of the outside lights shone, showing her the way in. It was well-lit and welcoming. She plodded up to the entrance and walked inside. There was no-one around, the ticket office was closed. Being early, she found the waiting room and entered. She needed somewhere to sit without thinking.

The waiting room seemed as dated as the station. Like the town, it was busy normally, but not at this time of night, and certainly not in this kind of weather. She went to the corner of the room, which was totally empty, apart from a table in the middle with a few travel leaflets on, as well as well-thumbed magazines. Old chairs and over-painted benches sat against the walls.

The centrally heated Victorian pipes seemed to speak, but if it was to Jan, she wasn't listening. Three radiators were pushing out a fair amount of heat. So much so, she was compelled to take off her jacket, which she then placed on the end of one of the radiators. Embracing the radiator for warmth, she watched as, from the jacket, the steam rose in pleasing shapes. Unfortunately, the jacket which she had acquired from a charity shop, didn't keep out the rain.

Jan was small, slim, barely 8 stone in weight and about 5 foot 3 inches tall. She looked almost child-like, even though she was in her late twenties. Her shoulder-length, black hair straggled across her face. She used her hands to push it back over her head, then the water dripped down her back, making her shiver. Now you could see in her eyes, on her face, the pain and the anxiety.

A man entered through the door. He was in his 50s, thin, good-looking, well-dressed, no raincoat and strangely dry. Straight away, he spoke to Jan.

"What an awful night! It's a long time since it's been this bad!" Jan dreaded the engagement. She didn't want to speak and, indeed, she didn't, but this only served to encourage the man. He was cheery, not the type to let others wallow alone.

"Are you from around here?" he said. Without pausing, he carried on talking about the area, the people, trains.

Jan kept her head down, moving her feet, which didn't quite touch the floor, in a figure-of-eight shape. The man stopped talking. Jan's feet carried on circling, then she was aware of the silence.

"My name's George. You know that's lucky?"

Jan looked up, her concentration broken.

"What's lucky?"

"The figure-of-eight. That's what you're doing with your feet." George gestured with his feet what Jan had been doing with hers. "Well, at least that's what the Chinese think," he added.

Jan was annoyed with herself for being made to speak when her silence sealed her away from the world. She looked down again, thinking it might stop George from talking; she was wrong.

Jan could feel her skin again, the warmth of the waiting-room slowly drying her off. George had picked up an old magazine, one that had been read a hundred times before by many other travellers waiting for a train. Jan lifted her eyes and looked across at him and said,

"My name's Jan."

She didn't know why but she felt compelled to say it. She found it somehow easier to talk, having warmed up.

"I haven't talked to anyone for a week. I've been sitting in my parents' house. My mum died from cancer recently."

There was a silence then George said,

"Sorry to hear that. How old was she, and how about your father?"

Jan replied, "My mum was 48, my dad left my mum when I was born."

George wanted to hug Jan. Jan wanted to be hugged. They remained seated. Another silence landed over the room. George, however, was not one to let things lie. He got up and walked round the room, humming to himself in the process.

He then spoke.

"In my experience, time is a healer, though it may not feel like it at the moment. Life has a way of pushing more important things at you, until these memories are softened, but never forgotten. I know you feel that nothing I say or that anyone else does, will help. It will ease, I promise you."

Jan looked up from where she had her eyes fixed. It was as if her body was trying to climb out of a big hole, but her legs were caught. She asked,

"What do you do?"

George was surprised that Jan had changed the subject, but he answered,

"I'm a loss adjuster."

There was a pause.

"So, you're an insurance man?"

George smiled.

"Yes, you could say that."

This tall man was feet away from Jan. She looked up. He somehow reminded her of a thin, gangly giant from a fairy tale.

He smiled down at her. In doing so, Jan realised that, while she had been talking to this man, her thoughts of her mum had taken a back seat. As you can imagine, it didn't take long for the feelings of loss to come back to wash over her.

It was silent again. George moved off and sat down. Jan looked up at the clock. There were twenty minutes before the mainline train would arrive. She got up and walked outside to the ticket office that had just opened. A few people had already bought tickets and were walking through to the platform. She bought hers and went back into the waiting-room to get her things. George was sitting down.

"Did you get what you wanted?" he asked.

"Yes," she replied, then continued, "Where are you going?"

"Nowhere in particular."

"Where would you like to go?"

He smiled, then said,

"What a wonderful question! Somewhere it isn't raining. Hot, but not too hot where you can smell the earth and hear the birds singing in the trees. A place where I could put my feet up and drink wine, feel the atmosphere, embrace it, and watch the sun travel across a turquoise sky, then watch the sunset, as I drop off to sleep, in the cool night air."

Jan sat down again, almost spellbound by his words. Not just by the words though, just as much by the look on his face and the way he spoke. Then she said,

"Can I come?"

"You can go anytime, just live your dreams! Don't think that they will end here tonight!"

"What do you mean?" she asked.

He continued, "If I'm not mistaken, you have bought a platform ticket for the main-line train to London. Not to meet someone or watch it go past, but to end your life by falling underneath it." The silence was tangible.

"Who are you?" Jan asked.

"Just somebody on a journey like you?" he replied.

The main-line train arrived then departed. Quite a few people had got off the train. Taxis came and went. George looked across at Jan and said,

"There's a taxi outside. Maybe you can continue on your journey now."

She smiled at him, slipped on her now very warm jacket and made her way to the door. George stood up. As she passed him, she wrapped her arms around him, nestling her head in his chest. He kissed her on the head. She looked up at him and said,

"I hope you find that place you spoke about."

"I'm sure I will now," he replied.

As she walked out of the room, she looked back. There was no-one there. For some reason, Jan thought little of it. In time to come, she would often think of George, and the reason why she didn't end her life, under the main-line train to London.

Ghost 2

A dream had filtered into Dara's head. He was sat in an easy chair, his head nodding backwards and forwards, as he slipped in and out of sleep. He moved into another position to get more comfortable. A dull traffic sound meandered through his thoughts, as the occasional car or truck went by.

Outside Dara's one-bedroom apartment, which was on the third floor in a block of flats, the day was slowly waking to a new year. Inside, Dara was barely alive and hardly awake. Perhaps a few electrical charges had reconvened but had then been extinguished.

Eventually, life found its way around his body and he slowly got to grips with his senses. He wasn't a drinker but had decided to drink a cocktail of spirits the previous night, New Year's Eve. He regretted it big-time. Dara felt ill-at-ease with his head. He took himself off to the bathroom. Another sound filtered through the wall from the flat next door. Their television was on. He guessed they must have been watching it as it turned midnight, for the fireworks. There must have been twenty, maybe thirty people in there. He was asked to go but, being bad company, he had decided not to. Anyway, he was punishing himself. He looked in the bathroom mirror and talked to himself, staring at his round, stubbly-chinned face, getting closer in order to look into his dark brown eyes. He took off his fashionable glasses, saying,

"You're not bad-looking! You're funny sometimes!"

A sense of darkness hit the pit of his stomach and tears filled his eyes. He was then sick as a dog.

It was difficult for him to conjure up a care in the world. He felt as dull as the day, even though it was New Year's Day. He went back to his chair by the window and tried to gather himself. He fell fast asleep, only to be woken up by people leaving the flat next door, calling "Happy New Year!" as they left.

Dara thought he could face a cup of tea, which he made in his tiny kitchen. The flat was perfect for one, for two, tolerable, so how they got twenty-odd people next door amazed him. He sat sipping his tea, whilst he pondered his life. The thing was, he had nothing to look forward to. His flat had remnants of trimmings from Christmas. A small artificial tree sat in the corner, its lights hanging limply. One bauble on the floor looked as lonely as he felt.

Two days before Christmas, his girlfriend of twelve months had packed him in unceremoniously. He was sat opposite her in a restaurant, surrounded by chatter; an air of expectation filled the room. Plans had been made for Christmas. He'd even thought of taking her to meet his mum in Bristol. In fact, that was what they were discussing when she suddenly said,

"Dara, I can't do this! I've met someone else at work. This guy asked me out and, well, I went out with him. We had a lot of fun."

"What do you mean?" he said. "*We* have fun! Only last week we went to my mate's 30th! You said you had a great time!"

"I did, that's true, but you didn't even dance."

"I'm no good at dancing! You know that, but I love watching you."

"You're dull, Dara! I want someone who can make me laugh!"

At this point, he wrapped his mind around a joke and told her it. She looked at him, shook her head, stood up and walked out of the restaurant.

He looked around his apartment. Maybe if he cleaned up the mess, the Christmas decorations, the tree... Instead, he clicked on the morning news. He just stared at the thousands of people who were celebrating the New Year the night before. He considered all the other people who, like him, were on their own, for whatever reason. He looked into the abyss only to see a fine grey mist. He felt vulnerable.

The local news came on. They started talking about being alone over the Christmas holidays and how neighbours should go round and make elderly people, who were all alone, feel better. He said, out loud,

"My God, what about the poor young fuckers, who've been dumped by their partners? Why not make sure they're ok?"

He switched off the tv and felt even more depressed.

Somehow, he felt cut off from everyone. His Asian roots had come adrift. The things he believed in now were just a mish-mash. Not that he was religious in any particular faith, but he now felt without home or family. He couldn't stand it anymore. He picked up his car keys, threw on some clothes and made his way out of the apartment, down three flights of stairs.

Party poppers and lonely bottles sat on the steps; remnants of another year passed. When he reached the bottom, he opened the door. It was quiet. He saw no-one. He clambered into his old Vauxhall Micra and drove off. The radio was on, the day was dark, but they promised sunshine later. Great, he thought.

It wasn't long before Dara reached the coast. He lived near an area of outstanding beauty. He sat in his car in the car park, a popular place for dog-walkers. There was a long beach, as well as high cliffs which you could walk along. As always near the coast, there was a strong wind and, coupled with rain, it meant that there were very few people actually walking. However, he was equipped. In the boot, he had weather-proofs. After all, it was one of the favourite things he used to do with Jade. They would often walk the cliffs together, even talking about getting a dog, but now he couldn't console himself. He started to cry. With the rain and wind outside, it seemed almost impossible not to. How long he sat there he wasn't sure. The sun crept from behind the clouds, the wind dropped, and he thought *fuck it.*

He started the engine. There was no barrier round the car park, just a big gravel surface, halfway up a field, which went either to the beach, or up to the cliffs. He drove the car up over the grass.

There was a sign saying Vehicles Not Allowed Past This Point. Ignoring it, he drove to the top of the cliffs. There was no-one around.

It was easy, he thought. *Just put my foot down, must be around a fifty-meter drop, leave my seat belt off. Even if the air bag went off, the impact would surely kill me.*

How does it come to this? How does the mind throw out all the good things and retain the bad?

His mind drifted, thinking of the impact of his suicide, how it might affect the people he knew. His mum was miles away and he felt, every time he saw her, how much she disapproved of everything he had done. His dad, whom he hadn't seen in a while, was in a home and didn't recognise Dara anymore. Somehow Dara and his sister had become estranged, as he hadn't talked to her for a long time. He thought of his extended Indian family but, somehow, the cloud that hung over him wouldn't allow him to see any of them clearly. As for his ex-girlfriend Jade, why would she care?

He summoned up the courage, the engine still running. He thought for a second, "Shall I go and see how far it is to the bottom of the cliff?" but that type of courage he didn't have. So, he put his foot on the gas and went for it. He was about 70 meters away from the edge. It seemed like an age before the car gathered up enough speed on the slippery grass, then, when he was less than twenty-five meters away, he saw a dog run in front of the car. He put his brakes on full, swerved to the right and stopped.

Dara got out of his car. He couldn't see the dog, he couldn't see anyone, in fact. It seemed desolate up there. Then, as he got out of the car and looked around, he had this ache in the back of his head. *Maybe it's a sign, but what sort of sign? Maybe to stop running over dogs on cliffs?* He then realised it must be whiplash from stopping so quickly.

Dara felt deflated. He walked back to his car, now bathed in sunlight, got back inside and became aware of something in the passenger seat. There sat a long-haired, very large golden Labrador, panting for all its might. Dara sat down carefully. *After all, he might be rabid.* He spoke to the dog, as you do,

"Hi there, I nearly ran over you!"

The dog's tongue lolled outside his mouth. Dara looked at his not unfriendly face. He lifted his hand to stroke the dog, who, in turn, lifted his head in appreciation of contact. The warming moment brought about more fussing from Dara, the dog enthusiastically rolling its head. A one-way conversation between Dara and the dog continued, as if he was talking to a human being, as all dog-owners do. The truth was, he had always wanted a dog, but had never owned one, so he didn't know what the etiquette was.

It was then he thought that the dog must be lost and must have jumped into the car because it looked similar to its owner's. He stroked the dog gently and found a collar with a silver disk hanging from its neck. On it, it said Sebastian. But no other details.

"Shit!" said Dara audibly. "What do I do now?"

It was then that he had a thought, not his thought, but someone else's.

"I'm not lost, I'm just out having fun! That was until you nearly ran me over."

Dara looked at Sebastian and said,

"Was that you, or am I going mad? I know I'm on the edge here, and I'm not in a fit state. What the fuck is this? Has someone drugged me? I don't believe in animals who can talk."

Again, inside his head, Dara could hear a voice.

"Shit pal, it's me! I'm communicating with you! I'm a good-looking dude with a brain that's more clued up than yours, so get your act together!"

As these words filtered through Dara's almost stagnant brain, caused by too much alcohol, as well as depression, Sebastian turned to Dara and licked his face, saying, in Dara's head,

"My oh my, your face tastes nice!"

Dara placed his hands on his knees, and said out loud,
"Let's be quiet so I can think."
Ten seconds passed.
"Well?" asked Sebastian in Dara's head.
"Well, what?" said Dara. "I need more time."
Immediately, Sebastian invaded Dara's thoughts.
"Look, as things go, you will get eight, maybe nine times longer life than me, so I ain't got time to sit and be savvy about every-thing you say." Sebastian continued, "Don't you get it? Even in our dreams, we dogs go running after most things that move. We ain't got the time to waste, pal."
Dara gave in to Sebastian interrupting his thought patterns.
"Why you here, why are you communicating with me?"
"I've got a job to do", Sebastian said, staring into Dara's eyes, which was not something dogs do normally, so Dara felt strange. He felt outside of himself, almost as if he could go and run after a ball, roll in some mud, or chase a cat. The elation wasn't lost on him; he saw in Sebastian's eyes the pure exhilaration of life. That, and the fact Sebastian was in Dara's head, made Dara see life differently.
"I've done my job. You're alive and now you have a reason to stay alive." Dara heard Sebastian, then said,
"Yes, you're right, it's clear to me now."

Unbeknown to Dara, a police car had pulled up next to him. A police officer got out of his car and walked over to Dara's car, whose door was open, then peered in at Dara who was in mid-conversation.
"Excuse me sir, but do you know you're not supposed to drive up here onto the cliff? It's extremely dangerous."
Dara jumped at the interruption, flustered as to what to say. Sebastian gave him a few ideas which Dara delivered without thinking.
"Hi dude! Yeah, we are here for the view. My friend Sebastian here asked me to come here to see the panorama, from up on the cliff."

The police officer said,

"Would you mind stepping out of the car for a moment, Sir?"

Dara got out.

"Have you been drinking, Sir?"

"No!" said Dara. The police officer asked him for his driving licence, then said,

"Would you mind breathing into this breathalyser, Sir?"

As Dara did so, he could hear Sebastian saying things in his head. *Tell the fuzz to fuck off, go and catch a real criminal!*

However, Dara tried his best not to repeat it. Instead, it was the police officer who spoke.

"Look, if you drive your car back to the car park or even go home and have a lie down, I'll let you off with a warning."

He then added, "I don't know if you're having a little joke or what, but there's nobody in the car, Sir, apart from you."

Dara quickly dipped his head to look in the car - Sebastian was there, as clear as day. He turned to the policeman, pointed and gestured, but somehow, he knew that he'd better just shut up and go. He got back in the car; Sebastian shot the words into Dara's mind.

Happy New Year knob-head! Dara delivered the words perfectly. Whether the policeman heard him or not, he wasn't sure. Dara felt ten feet tall.

He drove a few miles further down the coast, then stopped, just above another beach. Sebastian was quiet. So was Dara. Dara wasn't sure what to say, so he opened the car door and they both got out.

The only thing that came into Dara's head was,

"Why do dogs want to hump everything?"

Sebastian replied,

"Because it makes us feel good and because we can."

"Thanks Sebastian," said Dara.

"No problem pal," replied Sebastian, then added, "Listen to the word of Dog."

"Shouldn't that be listen to the word of God?"

As Sebastian ran off into the distance, chasing seagulls and barking loudly, Dara heard the words in his head.
Whatever made you think that God was human?
With that, Sebastian disappeared into the distance.

Ghost 3

"Can you make that two pepperoni pizzas with extra cheese, and a bottle of diet coke?"
"Yes sir!" came the reply, "Be there in twenty minutes!"

Max was on his sofa, watching TV. He loved sci-fi films. He was watching The Empire Strikes Back. He couldn't remember how many times he'd watched it. Not that it mattered; he knew it word for word. Max dominated the sofa. In fact, the springs had gone where his ample backside had sat on it for so long.
He lived with his mum in her semi-detached house, which she owned. She had converted the house into two separate flats. She lived in the one upstairs, so Max could have his own space downstairs, which was converted to Max's lifestyle. Some of the money for the conversion on Max's flat had come from the council, because of his inability to move around. His flat was one big room with a widened door, that led to the bathroom.
Along one end was his kitchen. A king-size bed sat at the other end, under the living-room window, with a big sofa in the middle of the room. On the wall sat a big screen tv, in front of which Max spent most his life. There were two small easy chairs in the room, as his mother would occasionally come and sit with him. Max now weighed 35 stone. He rarely went anywhere. Max wasn't happy. He was 25 years old, on benefits and large, too large! He had double chins and rolls of fat. Underneath all of this was a good-looking guy with fair hair, a cheeky infectious

smile, and a need to be thin again.

He hadn't always been fat, was never bullied at school, regularly part of the crowd. His personality made him popular. When he left school, he found his way into a company that worked in computers. Great at his job, he had won respect from his boss. He had a girlfriend, and they wanted to find a place to live together.

Two life-changing things happened in quick succession. First, his dad had a fatal heart attack, while he was doing some gardening and, secondly, within a week, his girlfriend was offered a job in America in the film industry. She was an actress, and it was too good a part to turn down. Sometimes he looked back and thought he should have gone with her, but he couldn't leave his mum at that moment and, in the months that followed, she would need him. As time went by, things were sorted out and he and his mum were beginning to get used to life again.

To begin with, Max and his girlfriend kept in touch by text and emails but, slowly, over time, this ebbed away. What had held him and his girlfriend together was gone.

Since then, he had seen her in the odd film in minor roles; she was beautiful and acted well. It had been five years since he had last seen her. She would not recognise him now. Slowly, over this period, due to his increasing depression, he got bigger and bigger.

The front doorbell rang. A guy came in with the pizzas. Max put up his hand. They shared hi-fives.

"Hey Joel!"

"Hey Max!"

They were together for a few moments, as Max set about his pizzas. Joel had a slice. They'd become good friends. Joel was a regular at Max's Big Film night, where a few of Max's friends came over, ate junk food and watched sci-fi films.

"When's the next Big Film night?" asked Joel.

"Next Friday," answered Max.

"Ok I'll be here! I'll bring a couple of free pizzas, spare ones."

They laughed. Joel left.

Max's other friends were two guys from school, both now married. Max had been asked to go to each of their weddings, but he'd kindly refused. He didn't want people looking at him and, of course, it was hard to get out of the house. Damn near impossible to travel.

Max's mother, Mary, was a short, thin, fiery woman with high cheek bones and a heart of gold. She let Max get on with his own life, still doing all she could for him, getting his food in, doing his washing. Being a big bingo fan, she went three nights a week. Having a pension from when Max's dad had died, it was more than enough to fund her obsession. She had had a few wins. Of course, the money had come in useful to help Max. Even so, he still needed his benefits which the social services were reviewing at this time. Max was worried that they may be reduced.

Things were getting to Max. His weight had always made him feel down, but what had brought him to here was losing both his dad and his girlfriend. He'd never been into drugs or drinking, but he had had anti-depressants, as well as sleeping tablets, for many years. Being so big made him irritable and tired. He was so close to giving up his life. Nobody knew how close he was, not even his mother.

There was a knock on the front door, then the bell rang. Max had dropped off to sleep, having watched a film in the middle of the night. He had drifted in and out of sleep all day, which was not unusual. It was about 4.30 in the afternoon, his mum was out, so he would use the intercom to buzz people in, once he knew who they were. The bell went again, and Max woke up.

He grabbed the intercom remote and said,

"Who's there?"

"Is this Max Caldwell?" It was a woman's voice. "Can I speak to you about benefits?"

Immediately, Max felt uneasy and annoyed that his mother wasn't in. He said to the woman,

"What's your name?"

"Joy," she replied.

"Can you come back another day?" he said.

"It's only an informal chat, nothing to worry about," she said.

For some reason, this seemed to convince Max, so he buzzed her in. Joy walked into the hall, then into Max's flat.

Max stared at the figure that was standing there, mostly in black: black trainer bottoms, black t-shirt, black hoody but, strangely enough, purple plimsolls. He was speechless for a moment and then said,

"Strange clothes for the social services!"

Under the hoody, a pale, white, thin, skeletal figure smiled. A look of shock crept across Max's face but, somehow, he kept his composure. Maybe watching so many science fiction films had helped but, inside, his blood ran cold. Joy said,

"Can I sit?"

Max didn't answer, he just stared. She sat down on the spare chair.

"You say your name's Joy?"

His voice quivered as he said it. She answered,

"Yes."

"You spoke about benefits," Max said, "but if I'm not mistaken, you're not here from the benefits agency."

Her cold dark eyes held Max, then she said,

"No."

Joy smiled. Not an unkind smile, one that made him feel more at peace with the conversation.

"I think we may have got our wires crossed here."

As she spoke, she removed her hoody. The surprise on Max's face was pure shock. Joy's arms were skin and bone, her hair like long, thin strands hanging down to her shoulders.

Joy was aware of his shock and it didn't surprise her. The air in the room was definitely cooler and Max could feel it.

"I..., I...," he stuttered, "I don't think you answered the question?"

"What was the question, Max?" Joy said slowly.

His mouth was open. He closed it, then said,
"I can't remember."

Max couldn't focus. In front of him, he saw death. Being a sci-fi buff, he'd seen many films that depicted it. It was a lot more frightening in real life. Eventually Joy spoke.
"What can you see Max?"
"I see a skeleton with skin, I see someone who should be dead, and yet you smile and seem kind. Are you here to take me? Am I going to die?"
"I did come to talk about benefits," Joy said.
Max immediately replied,
"Yes, that's it! That's it! That's what you said on the intercom! I thought you were from the social!"
"No, I'm here for your social welfare. The benefits I spoke of are your life." Joy continued. "My life was one of continuous abuse. What you see is what I did to my body. I ate too much, then made myself sick. I thought I looked ugly. Although my weight was normal, in the end I starved myself to death. We suffer from an illness Max; the only cure is to change."
Max lowered his head as much as he could. His chins refused to move.
"I know, but I've tried! I've tried diets! I've tried to be positive, but it seems hopeless."
Joy sat forward on the easy chair opposite him.
"Look at me, Max! Do you think I really wanted to be like this? I tried too, but it seemed hopeless. I drove myself to the end, like you are doing now, only there was nobody there who had already died from an eating disorder, to tell me."
Max looked at Joy. He couldn't believe she was real, or a ghost, or whatever she was, but she was there in front of him, and she looked like hell, in loose clothing.
"Why me then? Why are you here to help me?"
Joy sat back on the chair, still looking into Max's eyes.
"Because it was my choice and I picked you. We are the opposite ends of the scale, no pun intended!"

Max smiled. Joy continued.

"To tell you the truth, well part of it, you get to help me. We all need help Max, so save yourself for me!"

Then Max asked,

"Were you afraid when you died?"

Joy answered. "No, I was afraid of being alive anymore, because living seemed harder. Of course, now I know there's nothing more precious than life itself."

Then Joy got up, slipped on her hoody over her bony frame, turned towards the door and said,

"My favourite film was The Empire Strikes Back, the best film ever in my opinion."

Just as she slipped out of the door, she looked across at him and said,

"May the force be with you Max!"

Some considerable time later....

Max was sitting on his new sofa, between his two best mates. Joel walked in with two extra-large pepperoni pizzas in his hands. He looked straight at Max, then did a high-five to all three, before asking,

"How'd it go Max? Did you do it?"

Max's two thumbs, along with the huge smile across his face, gave the answer. He then said,

"I'm now under 20 stone! I've lost 15!"

"Wow!" was the reply in unison from his three mates.

"What with that and my mum winning £20,000 star prize at the bingo, life's looking good! My mum said if I lose another 5, she'll pay for my flabby skin to be cut off!"

All three of his mates hooted and shouted,

"High-fives all round!"

Max then said,

"One slice of pizza please."

They laughed.

"If you don't mind me asking, Max," said Joel, "what inspired

you to lose all the weight?"
Max pondered the question, then said,
"Let's just say, I found the Joy in living."

Ghost 4

The green beans were set and now starting to climb. The carrot heads were bright and standing in single rows, as were the beet-root. The outdoor tomatoes were staked, the earth was loamy, the manure heap turned. Harry's allotment was a sight to see. There were some that were unkept, others that were looked after, but Harry's was one of the best in the county.

Harry spent most of his days there, apart from when he was at home in his house with his own garden, where he grew his prized Dahlias and beautiful Azaleas, not to mention his green-house, where he brought on all his seedlings.

Harry was 67, thin, about 5 foot 10 inches tall and was still a good-looking guy for his age. When dressed for the occasion, he was quite dapper. His wife often said, as they were going out to the theatre, cinema, or sometimes even dancing,
"We do look so good together!"

Now Harry was all alone and had been for almost ten years. His wife had died unexpectedly, whilst he was at work. He was a train driver and was driving the night train from London to Edinburgh at the time his wife passed away. He received the news when he got to Edinburgh and, even though he was bereft with the loss, his first thoughts were to drive the train back to London. The management insisted that he must go home as a passenger.

Harry was happily married to Edna and they had twin girls, both in their first year at university. After she died, he had a month off from work. The girls came home and wanted him to have more time to get over his loss, but he refused, the girls went back to university and Harry carried on driving trains. Eight years later, at 65, he retired with a full pension. He was happy in his own way, the solitude suited him. He was methodical and almost mechanical. The soft side of Harry was his plants. That's where he found his peace. The care and attention he had to spare was given to them one hundred per cent.

The allotments didn't come up for newcomers very often, so when they did, there was, as always, a healthy waiting list.

A new face had taken one near to Harry's. Harry was very sociable, especially when it came to anything to do with gardening, so he spoke to all his neighbours and, four times a year, the allotment owners had a BBQ, where they all shared ideas and got tips on this and that. The odd person might show off or be an outright bighead about the size of their squash but, overall, it was usually a good night. Home-made damson wine would be drunk copiously; you could say a merry time was had.

At one of these events, Harry met the new guy, Peter, and they sat and talked. Harry found out that Peter, who had just moved into the area, was a psychologist, and it wasn't long before Harry was talking about Edna. That was when something broke in Harry. The conversation seemed to bring everything rushing up into his head. All the control and constraints were gone, and he started to cry. Maybe it was the wine. Of course, he made his apologies to Peter, who placed his hand on Harry's knee and said,

"Any time you need to talk, come and see me."

At home that night Harry cried like a baby.

It was spring. Throughout the winter, Harry had been kept busy, tidying his garden, briefly going down to the allotment to do the same. He had seen Peter a few times, as their paths crossed, but just a passing hello or a wave on a frosty morning. Now, however, it was full steam ahead. Harry was there every day, so was Peter, along with many others.

One day, Peter came over and said to Harry,

"Do you fancy a drink of wine at the end of the day?"

Harry felt tight inside his stomach, with fear welling up inside him, but he was a strong man, and he knew you can never hide away from life.

Harry walked down to Peter's allotment. The day had been fine. Harry was satisfied with his work on the allotment. Peter was already sat outside his shed, happily drinking some red wine. A small metal barrel close by, full of burning wood, was giving off a soft glow in the dimming light.

They greeted each other, exchanging a strong handshake, then spoke about flowers and vegetables. After this, Peter told Harry of his single life abroad, in France and Spain, being able to speak both languages. He had found translation work mostly among ex-pats, but also helping people with psychological problems. Peter said that he had come back for the normal life in Britain and especially the gardening. They talked with such ease; it was almost as if they had known each other for years.

Harry felt emotionally drawn towards Peter and he was sure Peter knew it. As the night came to an end, Harry was set to leave. Peter shook Harry's hand in the darkness, as the light from the embers of the fire faded. He pulled Harry towards him, hugged him and kissed him on the cheek.

Harry didn't resist. He felt something inside that had nagged at his conscience for years. They waved to each other and made their way home.

Harry thought back to when he was in the territorial army as a teenager. His best mate, Alfie Brooks, had shared a tent with him on the moors. They were with a platoon of other lads the same age. He and Alfie had drunk some beers they'd smuggled in with them. They both got a bit drunk. Alfie was always a bit effeminate, but Harry thought he just put it on and, anyway, homosexuality was not something you talked about much in those days. Alfie kissed Harry and Harry kissed him back.

Harry was entirely unaware of his own feelings. The next morning, they didn't talk. Harry was prostrate with contempt for the way he felt about himself and couldn't bring himself to talk to

Alfie.

The platoon had carried on with manoeuvres the following day, but Harry avoided Alfie. As the young boys were moving over some high ground, towards some woods, an officer came back through the trees. He called them to attention.
"We are going back to base to call the police."
A body had been found. Rumour had it they had found Alfie's body, hanging from a tree. Thoughts were that he had committed suicide, although officials said it was an accident.
Harry left the Territorials and tried to bury the memory. Years passed. He met Edna and they got married.

Harry spent all of the following day at the allotment, well into the evening. With Peter away at a conference, Harry's mind was in a quandary. The past had head-butted the present and he felt concussed. He busied himself through the day, into the evening, then he lit a Paraffin heater in his shed and sat on an old easy chair. Subdued light shone from a battery lamp.
Harry had come up with a plan. He had already written a letter for his daughters, explaining how he couldn't cope anymore and how he wanted to be with Edna.
Deep inside, however, he knew this was not quite the truth. His emotions had hit a crossroad; he could neither turn nor go straight ahead anymore, because of his feelings for Peter. So, this was his way out. The letter, he hoped, would help them feel better. Of course, he never mentioned his feelings for another man, but wrote, *after many years alone now, I thought it was time to go.* The truth was that he couldn't reconcile his thoughts with what other people would think, the shame it would bring on his family and, of course, the deepest memory of all, Alfie Brooks.

After writing his letter to the girls, he poured some tea from a flask and sipped it. It was still warm. He added some brandy for courage, then sipped it slowly.
The silence was interrupted by a sound outside. He picked up his torch and went out. He walked along to the end of his allot-

ment, where somebody seemed to be lurking in the dark. Harry shouted and told the person to bugger off. Harry got closer to the figure. He shone his torch at the person, who was now kneeling on the floor and asked if he was ok. Harry helped him up and carried him back to the shed over his shoulder, then sat him down on his chair. Harry looked at the young face. He saw a teenage kid in camouflage trousers and a jacket. He seemed ok, so Harry asked,
"Would you like a drink?"
The boy answered,
"Yes, Harry!"
"How do you know my name?" said Harry, before looking at his face again.
"Alfie!"
Harry passed out.

Harry was in his chair when he came round. He rubbed his eyes. Alfie was standing against the wall of the shed, then he said,
"I see you've been busy, Harry!"
Alfie was holding a noose in his hand. A look of shock still sat on Harry's face.
"How can you be here?"
A thousand questions were clicking in Harry's head; that was just the first one.
Alfie replied,
"You've been a lucky man! Nice life, lovely family! Sorry about Edna though, but all the same, you've so much to hold on to."

More questions jumped into Harry's mind. Alfie spoke before Harry did.
"No, I didn't commit suicide. It was an accident. I was sitting up a tree having a beer, waiting for the rest of you. I was practising knots. Stupidly, fooling around, I'd made a noose just like this one. I slipped it over my head. I don't know why. I lost my footing and fell. The rope got caught up in a branch and that was that."

"So, you didn't do it because of what we did?"

"Why would I?" said Alfie, "I had genuine feelings for you Harry. Maybe if I had lived, this would be a different story."

Harry put his head in his hands and cried. Alfie got down, pulled away Harry's hands from his face, then looked into Harry's eyes. "Promise me something Harry. Life is what you have today, not yesterday or tomorrow. If you feel love and, what's more important, if you get love back, surely, it's worth holding on to? After all, all you only ever have is now."

Harry awoke in the shed chair the next day. He had a blanket over his shoulders. He couldn't remember dropping off to sleep. He picked up the note that he had written, ripped it up and threw it into the bin. He stood up, then opened the door. The birds were singing, there were flowers on his French beans, the rhubarb was high, his allotment was beautiful. He stood in the early morning sunshine. At sixty-seven, he felt like a teenager again.

Across in the other allotment, he saw Peter, who waved and called over to Harry.

"Do you fancy a nice cup of coffee?"

Harry didn't hesitate. He closed his shed door and then made his way across to Peter's allotment.

Ghost 5

Aaron sat by the bedside of his mother Judith. She was in hospital suffering from dementia. Once she had been a vibrant, beautiful woman, light of heart and quick of brain but now, here she lay, this shell of what she had been before. Judith wasn't trying to cling to life. In fact, she didn't want to live anymore. She was in hospital because she had had a fall, cuts and bruises mostly. It could have been so much worse. Judith was found beside a railway track, her foot caught in the fence on an embankment.

The police had said to Aaron,

"Your mother told us she was going to Brighton for a holiday. Asked why she was wearing her nightdress and slippers, she'd replied,
"I bought them especially from John Lewis to get an even suntan."
Apparently, she had curtsied to the police constable and said,
"Can I kiss you? I love a man in uniform."

This had been a calm night out for Judith. There had been one time when she had just walked out of her house into the road, being missed by inches, as a car squealed to a stop. There had been countless other times she had walked out of her house, into danger.
Judith's love of trains went back to her husband, who'd been a volunteer on a steam railway. Many a time, Judith would ride on the footplate, as her husband drove the train. Trevor, her husband, had died five years earlier. Now on her own in a big house, she had a home-help every day, but they couldn't be there all the time. Aaron had decided to move back home and look after his mother, after his marriage had failed. His wife had left him after their business had gone bankrupt, caused mainly by his wife, who had spent all their profits.

The problem was, the bits Judith remembered, she held on to, but everyday living was just like walking through clouds.
Unfortunately, when Judith walked out of her front door, the mist descended and then she would be searching, trying to find her way back into her life. Now she lay in the hospital bed, a confused look on her face. Aaron gently stroked her hand. She looked at him and said,
"Who are you?"
This she had said so many times before, but Aaron understood. Aaron was steadfast, forthright and a good-looking man. Seeing his mum slowly slip away to this darkness that was dementia, made him question life.
Aaron had had his own problems with a failed relationship and

his business had gone under. He was not on good ground either, but at least he could determine his future.

A person was standing just outside the ward, looking in at Judith and Aaron. Head and face covered, this person was like a shadow against a wall. Doctors and nurses would pass by; they saw nothing. Visiting time was almost over. Aaron was making ready to go. An elderly man, wearing a dressing gown and with a blank expression on his face, was at the end of Judith's bed. As Aaron got up, the man said,
"Can I have some water?"
Aaron gave him some water in a plastic cup. The man threw it back at Aaron, soaking him, shouting,
"I don't want your fucking charity!"
A nurse arrived and ushered him away. Aaron was shocked. He felt sure that, like most the people on the wards, this man was suffering from dementia or Alzheimer's. Still drying the water off his coat, Aaron kissed his mother on the forehead, saying,
"Goodnight for now, mother."
She had gone to sleep. After Aaron had left, the person in the corridor went in and sat with Judith. At two o'clock in the morning, Judith awoke, puzzled, then looked at the strange woman. Judith stared at her and pleaded,
"Help me! I want to sleep and not wake up!"
She looked at Judith and said,
"I'm Sarah. I'm here to save you, not to take you."
"Then you're no good to me!" said Judith, now lucid, wide-awake and aware of her visitor. Judith seemed to know she was in the presence of someone not of this world.

Sarah was now confused as to the task she had been given.
She was one of five ghosts, who had each been given the chance to save the lives of five living people who were lost, confused, or unable to cope with life, and to give them a new path to live again. Their reward in return was a chance to return to the real world and live again, or to move on and not be caught in limbo.

Judith's mind slipped in and out of reality, her own confusion leaving Sarah lost for things to say to help her.

Hours went by, shifts changed. Sarah waited. She felt that, as long as Judith was there, she was safe, and she had a chance to save her.

The next afternoon, Aaron returned and sat with his mother. Every now and again, as he sat there, he was aware of a shadow through the glass in the corridor. He went to see what it was, but no-one was there.

Aaron sat by his mother's bed and remembered sunny days, when he would hold his mother and father's hands, walking across fields of wildflowers. As they walked, they'd swing him and, as he'd lift his feet, he would feel as if he was flying. The warm air and the smell of the dry earth had filtered through his senses and then, in the distance, he heard the sound of a train whistle. Now his mind was almost comatose, being so tired and worried. He felt at his wits' end.

Sarah stood in the corridor, watching. Time was her saviour.

Unlike mere people, ghosts have forever to wait. She became fascinated by Aaron. There was an air of sadness about him, even though she could see that the laughter lines on his face were deep.

It was late at night on the ward. There seemed to be peace, with all the patients resting quietly. Aaron slowly dropped off to sleep. Visitors were all long-gone. The nurses had seen him holding his mother's hand, as his head lay on the bed, so they left him to sleep there. Aaron's mother woke, looked at her son, smiled, then stroked his hair with her free hand. She closed her eyes and slipped away.

Sarah was caught by the stillness. She moved quickly to the side of Judith's bed, but she was too late. Sarah had failed to save Judith. She now stood opposite Aaron. As he awoke and stared at his mum, he looked at Sarah then again at his mum. He shouted, "Do something!" to Sarah, who was shocked that Aaron could see her. Apart from Aaron's mother, this was only the second person to ever see her. Aaron stared into her eyes and thought they were like two worlds, spinning in space. He was transfixed for a second. At this moment, Sarah felt that Aaron knew her own life-story. She stared back. They were caught in that place where lovers want to be.

She said the obvious.

"I'm sorry. There is nothing I can do to help your mother. She's passed away."

He looked at Sarah. Her face was etched into his mind; it was full of kindness. Aaron buried his head in his mother's hands and cried. Sarah put her hand on his head. She could feel the heat of his body. She felt alive. In the anguish of the moment, a nurse had turned up to take Judith's pulse. She comforted Aaron as best she could, as the nurse covered up his mother's face. Aaron said to the nurse,

"Where is the girl who was here a minute ago?"

The nurse said,

"There was no-one here when I came in. Perhaps you were dreaming."

At first, Aaron's emotions were confused, lost in a desolate place. Now he felt so alone, without anyone to share his grief.

It was late. He found himself by a coffee machine, mindlessly sipping the insipid brew, then he walked down a corridor, taking the first door. He needed to breathe fresh air. Instead of going down, he went up, as high as he could go. Eventually, he found a door that led to the roof of the hospital. The cold air hit him like a brick, his breath taken so suddenly that he fell to his knees. It had been raining but had stopped. There were puddles here and there. He wanted to cry; the tears wouldn't come but now his knees were soaked. He got up, realising he had no idea what the time was, or what day it was. It didn't matter.

The roof was flat at the edges of the building. A low, stainless-steel rail, about two foot high, sat on top of a small wall. Aaron got up and walked towards it. He stared out at the city land-scape. The sun was showing through the clouds. It wasn't warm, but it wasn't cold either. To him, it didn't matter. Aaron felt dead inside. He climbed up on the small wall and squinted his eyes at the sun, as it was uncovered by the clouds.

He contemplated his life. There was nothing logical about it.

It was irrational but he'd thought about it a lot and he couldn't see any reason why he should live.

A voice called Aaron. He looked back, grabbing the stainless-steel rail, because he felt unbalanced. Looking back, he said, "Sarah! Where did you go?"

"Nowhere," she replied. "I've been here all the time. What are you doing Aaron?"

"What does it look like? I'm going to jump!"

"Why?" she said, calmly, as she got closer to him. Please get down. Don't do it. You have so much to live for. Your mother wouldn't want you to give up your life."

Aaron felt sure there was nothing to live for. A few fine words from a good-natured, good-looking woman wouldn't sway him.

He moved his body closer to the edge, placing one leg over the stainless-steel bar. Sarah's task now seemed insurmountable. She accepted that she had lost his mum, that now, she would be lost in-limbo forever, but she felt emotionally attached to Aaron. She said,

"Listen, Aaron. I, too, have lost people. My husband and my child."

Aaron looked back at her.

"How?"

"In a car crash. I was driving late at night. I was tired. My husband was asleep, my baby in the back seat. I swerved to miss a deer in the road. I hit a tree."

"Oh my God!" Aaron said. He lifted his foot back over the rail, got down off the wall, and moved toward Sarah, wrapped his arms around her, then pulled back. She wasn't crying, but he was.

"How do you cope with that?" he asked.

"It happened many years ago. It has a place in my heart. It will always be there. Now I think they are happy."

A few moments of calm passed, then Sarah said,

"Would you like to go somewhere other than here?"

Aaron was relieved and said,

"Yes, I would!"

As Aaron walked through the door that lead from the roof, Sarah looked back. She could see four undefinable shadows, cast across the roof, as she left.

They found a café close to the hospital. They went to a quiet corner. There were only two other people in there - a woman serving and what looked like a homeless guy, sipping a hot coffee. Sarah sat down. Aaron got two hot chocolates, then he too sat down, having placed one of them in front of Sarah. Aaron looked into Sarah's eyes. They were a beautiful blue, but she had a red fleck in her left eye that made her look so unusual.

The homeless man looked across at Aaron, as he sipped his coffee. You could see on his face, that he was puzzled as he stared at Aaron. He spoke with a Northern accent.

"What's all this then? Who's tha talking to, me-lad?"

Aaron ignored him. So did Sarah. They continued to talk. Sarah did not touch her hot chocolate. The man at the other table continued to speak, as he poured whisky into his coffee.

"Are you all-reit?"

Aaron briefly looked towards the man, smiled, then carried on talking to Sarah.

The homeless man lifted his hands and made circles with his fingers in the direction of his head.

"An' they keep saying I'm crazy!"

Aaron's mind was somewhat lost as to what was going on, but things started to become clearer. Sarah carried on talking.

"My husband and daughter lived. I didn't."

Aaron's face was white, apart from around his eyes, where tears gathered. Sarah placed her hands on Aaron's and said.

"There's always something to live for. Life is precious! You must live it!"

Aaron turned again to the homeless man who was now swearing, noisily. When he turned back to Sarah, she had gone, disappeared.

An untouched hot chocolate left behind, it seemed as if he had sat there for hours. Everything that had happened went over in his head. He was lost in his thoughts. The woman who had served him came over and said,

"We are closing in ten minutes."

Aaron got home that night to his empty flat and slept fitfully. The next day, he went round to his mother's house. The large Victorian property seemed cold and lonely. He found it difficult, but he spent the rest of the day going through his mother's things. Old photos, his old room, still as he'd left it. There was a reason to live, not least to bury his mum and sort out all the personal effects.

His mother had a spot in the local cemetery where his dad was buried. As the days went by, he felt more comfortable in the house. His mum had left it to him and because she had not been placed in a home, it was free of any kind of debt.

Aaron made arrangements for the burial, then phoned to talk to Reverend Walsh, the vicar at his local church. She said she'd met his mother, Judith, briefly in hospital, on her rounds. Then she added,

"Can I say a few words about her? She was a wonderful woman. If that's ok?"

"No, I've no problem with that. Thanks." Aaron said.

There were a few distant relatives standing in the church and also some friends.

Aaron said some beautiful words about his mother and the vicar did likewise. Aaron was not a believer, but he wouldn't say he disbelieved either.

As he stood over the grave opposite the vicar, he looked at

her, without the pressure and pain that death brings, almost as if a veil had been lifted. He couldn't help thinking that she looked familiar to him, but he didn't know why. She had short, dark hair, a soft, light complexion, beautiful eyes. Back at his mother's house, the same few relatives stood around, talking solemnly. Eventually, he was standing next to the vicar, drinking a sherry. They were holding plates of finely cut sandwiches. They were all alone in a corner of the dining-room. Aaron asked, "How long have you been the vicar at the church?"

"Not long," she replied.

Aaron then asked,

"What's your Christian name? I don't know why, but I didn't catch it. Seems I've been in some sort of dream for the last few weeks."

She said,

"It's not unusual for you to be confused. It's a sad time for you, Aaron. I'm here to help. If you need me."

Then she added, "It's Angel, Angel Walsh. Yes, I know! A name that fits the job!"

Somehow, there was a strangely comfortable silence between them, then he noticed a red fleck in her left eye. For a moment, she felt self-conscious, because he was staring at her.

A silence lay across them like an invisible security blanket. A seemingly unspoken chemistry was exchanged. A sweet smile from Angel encouraged him to want to know more.

Angel asked about his mother and if he had someone he could turn to for family support. He explained he was presently going through a divorce, after his marriage had irretrievably broken down. He then asked,

"Why did you become a vicar?"

"Many reasons. They say it's a calling. My mother died in a car crash when I was a baby. Me and my dad survived, so it seemed to me, as years went by, that I needed a path, where I might help people. Being a vicar was perfect. After all, life is precious. We must make the most of it and live it."

On hearing this, Aaron's mind was in the clouds. All the things that had passed over the last few weeks were reconvening in this moment. He guessed she wasn't married, because there was no ring on her finger.

"Do you have a boyfriend or anyone special in your life?"

Angel could feel her skin flush. She looked down and played with her glass in embarrassment. After a few moments, she looked up into Aaron's eyes and said,

"Not at the moment."

Aaron smiled. The laughter lines on his face were full. They giggled like teenagers. Inside them, a fire was lit. A thousand butterflies seemed to rise out of their bodies and fly between them. An emotional rollercoaster had started, and their lives were about be lived to the full.

Five beings stood alone on a beach, in a place between here and somewhere else. Some would say they were ghostly; others would say they looked like standing stones, grey and lonely. One thing was for sure, if you got up really close and you were party to believing, these five figures were now free to live again, stay the way they were, or move on to that other place.

One of them looked up at the others and said,

"Not sure what you're doing guys, but I'm sure as hell up for chasing seagulls!"

HAPPY BIRTHDAY X

Through the letterbox, a few envelopes fell. Scat smelled them enthusiastically then ran backwards and forwards to the kitchen, trying to get Patricia's attention. She had heard the postman but loved Scat's excitement. Eventually, she went to the front door and picked them up; she knew they were birthday cards for her. She patted Scat on the head. At almost two years old, it would be Scat's birthday as well in two days' time.

Scat was a cocker spaniel that was a gift from Patricia's friends who had bought him for her, to keep her company when her husband Leonard had died. At the time, she'd thought it was the wrong thing for them to do, but as time went by, she and Scat became inseparable.

The day passed by uneventfully. Patricia was seeing friends at the weekend and having a little party, but today she was alone as usual. Scat was excited and ran round in circles. Patricia said "Walkies!" - that's all that was ever needed. Round the fields, down by the river, along the old railway track, a mid-afternoon tramp with her dog.

Patricia lived in a village where very little happened; no excitement, no problems, that's what was so nice about it. She never even locked the front door, but always checked to make sure it was shut.

Through the village ran a B road, albeit a quiet one. The village had a shop and even its own pub and a community hall. Its centre had hardly changed over hundreds of years, yet the edges of the village had new developments, added in a sympathetic way.

Her two-hundred-year-old cottage had been renovated over the years. Sitting beautifully in an acre of land with oak trees and a yew, it looked the perfect picture, well set-out with flower beds, bushes and shrubs, and, at one corner, a vegetable patch.

Patricia and her husband, Leonard, had lived here for 30 years, although, unfortunately, for the last two years, Patricia had been here alone, her husband having died at 63 with an early onset of Alzheimer's from which he had been suffering for several years. Patricia had retired at 59 to look after him. Now 65, two years after his death, she was still trying to get by without him. She would hear his words comforting her, "You look great gal!" Then she could almost feel a ghostly arm and a peck on her cheek.

She would often stand and look at herself in the full-length hall mirror, as her cocker spaniel sat at her feet, moving his head from side to side, thinking she was talking to him. Sometimes, she would even pick-up Scat's front paws and go waltzing round and round in the hall. This was adored by Scat, who, afterwards, would run round and round in circles with excitement.

At 65, she looked after herself, attending local exercise classes at the community hall, so she looked in good shape. She was of medium height, her swept back hair greying, but sensitively dyed to ease the ageing process. She was good-looking; she and Leonard had made a smart and engaging couple. Now, as a single woman, she was still very attractive, with the odd eccentricity, that gave her a more charged look: bold scarves, patchwork leather boots, hats from her trips abroad with Leonard, things which made her stand out in a good way.

She slipped out of the front door, checking it was closed, her dog, Scat, already pulling on his extending leash. She waited till she got to the front gate, then corrected the dog's enthusiasm. Patricia unhooked the gate, whose opening was over-hung by ivy and roses which intertwined in a curvaceous arch.

It was late February, so no real colour yet. In the summer, the garden and the hedges were a riot of colour, mostly due to the hard work of Leonard over the years, and of course Patricia's obvious encouragement.

She turned and walked along the lane, where she was greeted by many hundreds of snowdrops along the roadside; here and there, bunches of daffodils awaited to spring to life.

She made her way on the narrow footpath to the main road, where she then turned again through a gate, then into a field. Here on in, up to the old train track, Scat was free to run; no cows, no sheep, just wonderful smells for him to chase and investigate. These moments were the best for Patricia's mind.

Her thoughts would go backwards and forwards, examining her life, her time with Len, the laughs, the tears, the kisses, the love; she missed it all, but just to have one hug of reassurance, every now and again, would have made the pain so much easier.

Even when Len was ill, she could hug him, kiss him, and most of the time he would reciprocate, albeit with a question in his eyes.

Strangely, that day, she saw some sort of hawk in the sky, the type of which she was unsure, but she was stunned by its beauty, gliding over the trees, no doubt looking for an easy prey. Patricia stood still. Scat ran way off ahead, enjoying himself.

As the bird came lower and lower, she thought of taking out her phone to take a photo, but she didn't want to scare it. It landed on a telegraph pole, no more than ten meters away, settled, then watched. She could see its eyes looking at tufts of grass about five meters from her. She felt rigid, praying for Scat not to come back yet; within seconds, the bird swooped to the grass. Patricia caught her breath and a tear rolled down her cheek. She heard the squeal of what must have been a mouse. The bird looked at her, with an almost triumphant look on its face.

The bird spread his wings, just as he was about to fly off. Scat came charging over the fields, almost as if his mistress was a damsel in distress.

The majestic bird was long gone, mouse in claws, by the time Scat arrived. The way he barked and got excited, you would think he had saved Patricia's life, but it made Patricia smile.

The old train track stretched out ahead. Even with brambles and fallen trees, you could still see for miles that it was straight as a die both ways. Scat was back on the lead, because, on one side of the track, horses were kept; anything alive would have to be chased by Scat.

Patricia and Scat got to the old station, where she stopped and listened, as she used to do with Len, when he was alive, to see if they could hear a ghostly old steam train coming down the line. She waited. Scat sat still by her side, almost as if he knew what she was listening for. She looked down at her dog and said, "What an old fool I am, Scat."

Scat's tail shook wildly, then she heard an owl. It was getting near twilight and a strange glow sat over the trees, as the sun was setting. A mist gathered in the well of the old track. She stayed still, almost bolted to the floor, then a breeze cut through the mist like a knife, leaving her holding her chest, as she audibly let out a loud sigh. The dog started barking; she shooshed him, and then said, "Let's go home."

She walked quickly up the side of the track, with the road

bridge crossing over it. An old red phone box sat next to the bridge, with ivy growing up through it. Several of the glass panels were cracked or broken, the ivy winding its way round the inside of the box. Many coats of red paint were peeling off the outside. As she was passing, she heard a phone ring.

She looked in her pocket but, hearing nothing from her own phone, she stepped towards the phone box. She opened the door with difficulty, as it was very stiff. It was dark inside. The phone rang again. She kept her foot on the door to prop it open, whilst Scat sat dutifully outside, then she picked up the phone. Silence. She said, "Hello."
She heard a man's voice say, "Is that you?"
She said, "Who is this?"
"It *is* you, isn't it?"
Again, Patricia repeated, "Who is this?"
"Patricia, have a lovely birthday!" came the reply, then the phone went dead.
Her foot slipped from the phone box door, she pulled Scat in with her. Feeling frustrated and scared, she put the phone down, only to pick it up again and realise the line was dead. A few moments passed with Patricia feeling strange in the darkness, then suddenly the light in the telephone box came on.
After what seemed a lifetime, yet was in fact moments, she pushed the heavy door open. For some unknown reason, it was easier to open. Everything seemed different. As she walked, she thought about the voice; it was strange yet familiar and what did It mean? It wasn't her birthday today. Patricia made her way down the road, past all the houses in the village, till she reached her cottage. It was most rare for her to be out this late. The street lighting was strange and unfamiliar; she had never realised that it was so dull. She went through the gate, thinking the security lights would come on. She cursed when they didn't, reached the front door and let herself in.

This was when she stopped dead.

She looked at the hallway where everything seemed dated, the lighting dull. For a moment, she felt she was in the wrong house. There was also a strong smell of pipe tobacco in the house. Looking around, she noticed the hall mirror was missing.

A male voice said, "Who is that?"

A man walked into the hall, holding a newspaper in one hand and a pipe in the other, looking over his reading glasses. He must have been in his early forties.

"Can I help you?" he said, but Patricia stared at this man, speechless. She heard another voice and then a woman emerged from the kitchen, wearing an apron and carrying a rolling pin covered in flour.

"What's the matter, dear?"

The man replied, "There appears to be a lady in our house, and a dog."

Patricia fainted. When she came round, they managed to help her into her kitchen, or to be precise, someone else's. The man and woman were staring at her; just outside the kitchen door, two smaller faces, clearly children, stared as well.

The woman sat down opposite Patricia and held her hand. Patricia looked around the kitchen, which had a quaint air about it, feeling warm and tidy, with a beautiful smell of bread being made. Everything seemed to call out 1950s. Patricia thought carefully before speaking, pinching herself to see if it was a dream. It was not.

Meanwhile, the man with pipe had called the local police station in the village. Patricia said,

"I thought this was my house! I must have made a mistake."

There was a knock on the front door. When the man came back from the hall, he was accompanied by a policeman, who immediately took control.

"Right, madam. Can you tell me your name?"

"Patricia." she answered.

"Your last name?"

"Johnson."

"Where do you live?"

Patricia was about to say "Here", then checked herself.

"I don't know."

The policeman looked away.

"Mr. and Mrs. Fisk, I think I'd best take Mrs. Johnson to the police station." Patricia felt dizzy. Whilst this is was going on, Scat was being played with in the hall by the children. Patricia took another look around the room. Despite feeling in shock, she did notice a calendar on the wall. It said 1950.

The policeman asked Patricia to go with him. She felt that half her brain was somewhere else and indeed it was. Mrs. Fisk looked kindly at her. As she walked through the hall, the children gave Patricia the dog's lead. Patricia looked at them and smiled; they looked and smiled back. Patricia had always loved children, especially as she couldn't have any of her own. She asked them their names and how old they were.

"I'm Luke and I'm 10."

"I'm Shirley, I'm 8."

The policeman looked at Mr. Fisk.

"Where's your other daughter, Louise?"

Mr. Fisk hesitated but Mrs. Fisk responded,

"She's upstairs. She doesn't feel very well."

"Oh," said the policeman. "Well, hope she gets better soon."

At the front door, Patricia turned and looked back into the hall, thinking,

"It's my house!" But the time was not hers; she said nothing as she walked away, with the policeman holding her arm. She heard the front door of the house close.

Patricia said, "Where are you taking me?"

"A short walk down the road to the police station."

"There's a police station here?" she asked.

"Of course! Why not?" he replied.

As they turned towards the centre of the village, Patricia felt a rush of blood to the head, pulled away from the policeman and ran in the opposite direction, with Scat also in full flight. All she could hear in the distance was the policeman shouting, "Come back!" then, moments later, a whistle.

Patricia ran as fast as she could to get away. In the darkness, she was lucky not to fall, but Scat eagerly pulled her forward and, before long, the light of the phone box loomed in the darkness. She pulled the door hard, but it opened easily. She stared at the old black handset and felt confused. Fortunately, the light inside the box made it easy to see, so she lifted up the telephone. It suddenly went dark. She knew she was back in the present time, because of the smell in the telephone box.

She closed her eyes for a moment, then opened them and looked down at Scat, who seemed as happy as ever. She leant against the door which was stiff to open, walked out into the darkness and saw the streetlights, bright and welcoming. She hurried home in the dark. As she opened her front gate, the security lights came on, she walked to the front door, opened it and entered her house.

That night, Patricia slept fitfully, yet sound enough, and was woken by Scat licking her hand. She remained lying in her bed for a while, then pulled herself up to sit. Looking around the room, the warmth of the decor made her feel secure, so she took her time to rise from her bed, with thoughts of the night before constantly on her mind. She went downstairs, stood and looked at herself in the hall mirror and talked to her reflection.
"Well, what was all that about, Leonard?"

You couldn't make it up. Her hall felt more roomy, light and airy, in comparison to the one she remembered from the previous night. Of course, now, the sun was shining through windows in the house so it would be more pleasant anyway. She walked into the kitchen and looked through the large window at her lawn and flower beds. The kitchen was bigger than that in the other house, having been extended by Patricia and Leonard when they moved in, but Patricia could remember how it used to be.

Patricia made herself breakfast and sat sipping her coffee, going over in her mind what had happened the night before. Before long, her curiosity peaked, she needed to know more. In her working days, she had been a researcher for a solicitor, so investigating came naturally to her.

It wasn't long before she had lists: the village, her house, the people and their lives. Yet one thing that kept coming back into her mind, was the phone call, the phone box and, even more strangely, the voice.
Patricia looked out at the beautiful morning, the birds already camouflaging the bird table, the air still a cold chill, with frost on the lawn.

Patricia dressed herself. She looked different, having searched her wardrobe for clothes that would suit the 1950s. Scat watched her and seemed to approve. She made her way downstairs, in search of Scat's lead. When she found it, Scat became excited, especially as she got down on her knees and fussed him, saying,
"Sorry, Scat! I have an overnight stop for you at my friends."

Patricia drove Scat to her friend's house, not far away in Hereford, and explained,
"I'm going for an overnight stop with my niece. I'll be back late tomorrow night."

She drove back home. As it was still a beautiful day, she decided to walk around the garden, reminiscing how she and Len would have spent hours out there, gently tending it over the years, creating a small masterpiece.
Back in the house, looking for her handbag, she glanced at herself in the hall mirror. Her appearance was very much like that of a woman from the fifties. Luckily, she always did have a sense

of style.

She faced herself again in the mirror, then spoke,

"What do you think, Len?"

She could hear his voice in her head, always positive, always comforting, "You look lovely, sweetheart!"

Only when the dementia got bad did he lose that attitude; then and only then, she saw confusion and muddle.

She opened the front door, stepped out into the sunshine and started to walk. It seemed strange not to have Scat by her side, but she knew she couldn't do this with him. She made her way around the fields, where the ground, fortunately, was firm from lack of rain and a hard frost, glad that she was wearing sensible shoes. She went down to the old railway track, then up to the station, where she paused.

She had always stopped here. There were times over the years when she and Len would come here with a picnic. They'd sit on the embankment, dreaming dreams, all of which contained the children they so wanted. Eventually, they found out they couldn't have any, so resigned themselves to enjoying life without them, but it never stopped them pining.

Of course, they never stopped trying; there were times, on wild summer nights, that they would find themselves enjoying the passion of outdoor lovemaking, whilst ensuring that they were always discrete, so this beautiful spot held many wonderful memories for Patricia.

She carried on walking up the slope to the bridge, the road and the phone box. It then hit her. What if nothing happens? What if it's just some sort of crazy dream. She waited outside the phone box, hoping the phone would ring, but nothing happened. With difficulty, she pulled open the door and stepped inside. It felt claustrophobic, damp and certainly not nice.

The telephone then started ringing. She waited, looked at the push button phone, picked it up. She felt compelled to close her eyes, then jumped with shock, as someone tapped on the phone box door. She turned and saw a woman holding a baby, Patricia felt emotional and pushed open the door with ease, as the woman said,

"Are you alright, dear?"

Patricia looked at her and said, "Yes I'm ok".

The woman with the baby said,

"It looked like you were crying."

"Oh sorry," said Patricia, "There was something in my eye."

"That's alright then," replied the woman.

"Have you finished with the telephone? Only I need to ring my sister."

Patricia quickly replied,

"Yes, yes fine! I'm done!"

The woman bundled herself and the baby into the phone box.

Patricia took a sharp breath of 1950s air. The sun was shining, and she smiled to herself.

She stood and looked down the road, left then right. On her right, the bridge stood over the train track. A sign on the wall said Holmeworth Station; to her left sat the station house.

She started to walk slowly down Old Bridge Road, the road where her house was, on the right of which was a junior school. She saw children just starting to file into the playground out of the classrooms, for morning break.

The school didn't exist anymore. In *her* time.

An architect in the 1960s had built a big house, sympathetic to the area, to replace it; behind it, where the old playing field was, more houses had been built, by the same architect, again very sympathetically.

She started to walk towards her house, the one that now belonged to the Fisks. On the right sat the church hall, right next door to the old church, with, further up, on the left, a row of shops - a newsagent, a grocer, and a butcher.

She looked in the butcher's window as she went past, noticing the beautifully laid-out meat, pheasants hanging in the corners of the window. She looked up and the butcher lifted up his straw hat to her and smiled. She smiled back, then carried on walking.

In her time, there was now only a newsagents / convenience store, nothing else.
Further on, a couple of young women walked towards her, arms linked, with scarves over their heads. They looked at Patricia, who became instantly nervous, feeling that they must know she came from a different time. She wanted to cross the road, but they merely said, "Good morning!" and walked on by. Eventually, she came to her house on the left; a track ran along the side of her house, instead of the road which lead to the new houses.

She looked carefully at her house, now Mr. and Mrs. Fisk's house. But for a few things, there was little that was different, and it pleased Patricia that the village was a picture, then, and still was.

Now, she needed courage. She walked up the path with its burgeoning daffodils and snowdrops under the trees, breathing in as much of the air as she could. There was no bell, but there was an old knocker. She knocked twice. There was a delay, so she knocked again. The door creaked open. Standing there in her pinafore and holding a dish cloth, Mrs. Fisk said,
"Can I help you?"
For some reason, Mrs. Fisk seemed smaller, almost tiny.
"Do you recall me from the other night?" asked Patricia. "Patricia, Patricia Johnson. I'm sorry, I barged into your house, I have come to apologise."
"Oh!" said Mrs. Fisk, "It's no problem!"
There was a pause, then Mrs. Fisk said,
"But the Constable told us you ran away!"
Patricia thought for a second, then said,

"No, I think he got that wrong. I walked home."
Mrs. Fisk looked confused.
"I mean," said Patricia, "I simply got off at the wrong station in the dark, and made a mistake, thinking this was my house."
Patricia wanted so much to go into the house again. She said, "Do you think I could have a drink of water?"
With this, Mrs. Fisk invited her in.

Patricia was again seduced by the walk back into the past of her own house, the smell of tobacco smoke and what seemed like bread being baked. It was like a drug and Patricia felt light-headed. Mrs. Fisk asked her through to the kitchen, obviously so much smaller than Patricia's modern extension. Mrs. Fisk's was so warm and cozy and had its own charm, with kitchen implements hanging from the ceiling. The warming sun was hitting some of the pots and pans, as she walked in.
"Sit down!" Mrs. Fisk said, "Tea?"
"Yes please!" replied Patricia.
Mrs. Fisk seemed slightly agitated, as she heard a voice,
"Mum, mum!"
It seemed like a slightly pained call from somewhere in the house.
"Excuse me a moment," said Mrs. Fisk, as she left the room.
Patricia moved towards the door to see if she could hear anything; other than whispering, she heard no clear words. Patricia sat back down. The kettle, sat on an old black range fuelled by wood, started to whistle. In fact, the sounds and smells left Patricia intoxicated and she jumped when Mrs. Fisk walked back in.
"How is Louise?" she asked. Surprised by the question, Mrs. Fisk stumbled over the words,
"She's fine."
Then, almost as if she wanted to say something, Mrs. Fisk seemed to bite her lip and remained silent. She then smiled and asked,
"Do you take sugar?"

"Yes, I do!" replied Patricia. "How old is Louise, Mrs. Fisk?"

"14," Mrs. Fisk answered. Apart from the occasional "yes" and "no", Patricia felt that she was not wanted in the house, so she finished her tea and made to go, thanking Mrs. Fisk for her hospitality.

As she walked into the hall, she turned her head to see the back of someone in a dressing gown, going up the stairs, then turning slightly to look back. Patricia wasn't a hundred percent certain, but this 14-year-old girl was either quite plump or very pregnant.

At the front door, Patricia thanked Mrs. Fisk and asked her what her first name was, despite already knowing from the little research that she had already done. But Patricia thought it polite to do so.

"Maud."

With that Patricia said, "Hope to see you again," and, almost as an after-thought, Maud said,

"That would be nice."

The door closed behind Patricia, leaving her so curious as to what was being hidden. Of course, it was nothing to do with her, but then she thought, so why am I here?

After this, Patricia needed thinking time, so she walked around the fields, the 1950s fields. Without Scat it was quiet, but it gave her food for thought. As the day was still fine, sitting in the house gave Patricia a sort of lost-in-time feeling; now she was free, out in the fields, living life as it was 68 years ago. Nature had left no harmful mark, unlike people.

Eventually, she came to the railway track and noticed an amazing difference. There was a little siding, upon which were an engine and some coaches. There were a few railway people doing maintenance on the track, which she looked down upon, as the railway track sat below the tree line. She stopped and waited, absorbing the long-lost era.

A short while later, she continued walking, down to the station, then along the station platform, where the station master said, "Good afternoon!"
Patricia asked if it was ok to sit on the bench. He looked at her, surprised, and replied,
"Of course, my dear!"
These words of endearment had been lost in time. He asked if she was waiting for someone; she hesitated, then said,
"I might be."
He left her in peace.

She sat on the bench in the afternoon sun, where her mind floated in a bubble of reminiscence, the very place where Len would be by her side, more or less in this spot, in years to come.

Not long afterwards, she snapped out of her dreaming, as a train whistle was sounded and a train approached the station. She watched the engine as it gently brought the coaches in to the platform; there was a great rush of steam, as the brakes brought the whole train to a halt. She watched transfixed as the station master opened a door or two, and, as a few people alighted, she wanted to pinch herself, feeling blessed to be experiencing this long-lost past.

As the train had merely paused on its journey south, a few more people got on. In the world that Patricia was in at the moment, there were just a few people she had interacted with. Other than that, this world was going on and on, without any knowledge of her journey back to it.
As the train pulled out, the power and energy gave her a need to find out more; what was going on and why was she here and how was she involved? The train moved away under the road bridge, causing the steam from the engine to make the bridge look as if it were floating in mid-air.

Patricia got up off the bench and walked up the slope towards the station house, the road and the telephone box. When she got there, a man was inside making a call. She noticed it was Maud's husband, Frank. She moved closer, so she could hear, taking care not to let him know she was there.

She heard him mention a meeting with someone, saying a name at the end, just before he put the phone down, but it wasn't clear enough to be sure of.

As Mr. Fisk left the phone box, Patricia faced the opposite way, so he couldn't see her face, but she had no need to worry; he walked away quickly down the road to his house, leaving Patricia thinking, "Why did Mr. Fisk use the telephone box, when he has a phone at home?"

Patricia pulled the door open and stepped inside. She picked up the phone. She closed her eyes. She didn't know why she did it. It just seemed like a nervous response to the event that was going to happen.

Before Patricia opened her eyes, her nose told her she was back, the damp horrible smell permeating her head. It was late afternoon, and she was tired. One thing she did find was that the event had knocked her energy levels. She got into her house, decided to have a sherry, sat at her computer with all good intentions to do more research on the Fisks but by 7 o'clock, she was in bed and fast asleep.

She awoke the next morning to rain lashing at the windows and a dark foreboding sky, an ideal day to do some hunting, she thought. She had to pick up Scat late afternoon, so she made herself a hearty breakfast of bacon, eggs and tomatoes, followed by a coffee, then started on the computer.

Before long, Patricia had traced the Fisks' children and their family tree, which showed Shirley, their youngest daughter, had married when she was twenty, she had had two children, a boy and a girl. Luke, their son, didn't marry, but he had a relationship with a girl, and they had a boy. Louise got married at twenty-three and had twins.

Patricia made a file and printed it all off, but she felt there was something else that she was missing. Her female intuition told her that, judging by their behaviour, the Fisk parents were hiding something.

She decided to go and get Scat from her friend's house. As she drove over the bridge, in the village, she noticed something attached to the telephone box. She pulled in quickly, without signalling, almost creating an accident, as several cars honked their horns and numerous rude gestures were sent in her direction. Patricia stared at the notice attached to the telephone box.
"This telephone box is no longer in use. All equipment will be removed."

The date was in two days' time.

Patricia turned her car round, went back home and called her friend on her landline.
"Hello Jane! Could you keep Scat for one more night? Only I've just been asked by my niece to her friend's birthday party."
Without a second thought, Jane replied,
"No problem! Scat's great, we are having so much fun with him!"
Patricia said,
"Thanks so much!" and put the phone down.

The following morning, the skies were grey. It was Patricia's birthday and rain had been promised. She made herself ready, even remembering to take her mobile phone, as she wanted to take a photo of the old house. With no time to talk to Len that morning, all she said, as she left the house, was,
"Wish me luck, Len!"

Within five minutes, she was at the telephone box. It seemed that the door was getting stiffer. She immediately picked up the phone, she didn't close her eyes, but then she felt dizzy, so she felt she had to.

She opened the door easily. It was pouring with rain, so she reached into her bag and pulled out a telescopic umbrella, which was multicoloured and very noticeable. She cursed herself, but no matter.
She hurried down the main road as fast as she could. It was then that she realised it was Sunday; she'd lost all track of time, the shops were shut, the road was dead. It wasn't long before she reached the house, just as another thought came to her. Everyone will be home.

She stopped, had a quick re-think and walked down the track. At the side of the house, there was an old shed in the back garden, with just a small fence separating her from shelter. Patricia fell over the fence, but luckily she didn't hurt herself. Slightly damper, she pulled the shed door open, only to find spiders' webs everywhere. She never feared them, so she simply wafted them away with her umbrella. She cleared cobwebs and dust from the glass and looked towards the house.

Up to now she had considered all the angles, but this was a last-minute bid to find out what was going on. She could see Maud in the kitchen window, seeming to be washing up. Patricia looked up at the bedroom nearest the shed. She could have sworn she saw a girl! It must have been Louise; she was holding something in her arms.
It was then Patricia knew the secret, but she needed to be 100 percent certain, but how the hell could she just knock on the door on a Sunday and do that?

And then she heard it. The church bell rang. This, at first, meant little, as it had always rung for service on a Sunday. Patricia, not being particularly religious, never partook, unless invited to a christening or wedding. She watched and waited and hoped against hope that the family might go to church, and, sure enough, she saw movement down the side of the house. She ventured out of the shed and stood by the corner of the house. As she peered around it, she saw and heard the children.

Then, Mr. and Mrs. Fisk moved out of the garden and crossed the road to the church. By now the rain had stopped. Now, Patricia stood a chance. She walked round to the front door and opened it, stood in the hall and breathed deeply.

As she gathered herself, she knew she didn't want to frighten Louise, so she knocked gently on the wall, and called Louise's name.

"Hello Louise! It's Patricia! I called the other day and saw your mum!"

Then Patricia took a chance and said,

"Have you had the baby? It's alright, I mean you no harm."

Slowly down the stairs a little girl, who must have been no more than five foot nothing, appeared, carrying a tiny baby wrapped in a pink shawl.

Patricia moved forward, to see her and asked,

"When did you have her?"

Louise hesitated, then replied,

"In the middle of the night."

Patricia put her hands forward and said,

"Oh my God, you poor thing! But she's so beautiful."

Then she helped Louise into the kitchen. Louise sat down by the range with the baby on her lap. It seemed like a baby holding a baby to Patricia, as she sat right opposite Louise on an old wooden chair.

"I remember you from the other day. I don't know why, but there's something familiar about you," said Louise.

"Yes," said Patricia. "I'm a very old friend of the family. I've been trying to get close to your mum."

Louise looked concerned.

"Will I get into trouble?"

"No, of course not! I'll tell you what! Let's make a pact, just between you and me! I tell no-one and you tell no-one."

Louise thought for a moment. They shook hands, then they hugged, seeming so natural together. Patricia even got to hold

the baby, a moment she would never forget. She asked,
"Have you been here, keeping this secret, for nine months?"
Louise replied,
"No, I have been living at my aunt's until recently. At first, when mum and dad found out I was pregnant, they went crazy and sent me there. I've only been back a week, as my aunt was taken to hospital, after she fell and broke her leg. She couldn't look after me anymore, so I was brought back here in the dark. No-one knows! My mum told everyone I was working in a big house and living in."
Patricia looked at Louise.
"What's going to happen now?"
"Someone is going to have my baby," said Louise.
"Who?"
"I don't know," replied Louise.
"How do you feel about it, Louise?"
Louise burst into tears.
In the warmth of the old kitchen, a small friendship opened up between this young girl and the older woman.

As Patricia was holding the baby, Louise could go to fetch a handkerchief. Patricia quickly got her phone out of her coat pocket and took a photo of herself and the baby. For a few minutes, Patricia was feeling in her element, and didn't want this time to end, but the time went by so quickly. Patricia was worried about the phone box, about Louise, about the baby. She also knew she had no right to be there, but then again why was she?
Her educated guesses were of a jigsaw puzzle; she had all the pieces, but now she needed to put them all together.
She also realised that the last thing she wanted was to cause trouble between Louise and her mum and dad if she were to be caught there.

Patricia said that she would have to go but, before she did, she said to Louise,

"Please name your baby and make sure that whoever has her keeps that Christian name."
Almost as an after-thought, she added,
"Give something from you to go with the baby, a teddy, a doll, so she'll know who you are, she'll have your smell."

Louise looked at Patricia and said,
"I have nothing like that."
She stood there in the hall, this small vulnerable child, holding a tiny baby and a handkerchief.
"Is that your handkerchief?" asked Patricia.
Louise said, "Yes, I embroidered my initials on it."
"Then pass that on with your baby. Maybe one day she will come to find you."
As she spoke, Patricia had neared the front door.
They exchanged the warmest of hugs and kisses, almost as if they had known each other for years. then Patricia stepped outside and waved goodbye. As she crossed to the other side of the road from the church, she noticed Mr. and Mrs. Fisk and the children talking to other parishioners outside the church. Patricia walked quickly, head down.

The weather was now fine. It wasn't long before she got to the phone box, went inside, looked back over her shoulder at the village, thought about a thousand things she should or could have done, but realised how lucky she was to be there at all. A few seconds later she was back in her own time.

It was late afternoon before she relaxed. Patricia sat in front of her computer, but there was little to find there; her thoughts, her questions were altogether elsewhere.

Quite some time ago, Patricia's parents had both died in their late seventies. They had been inseparable and loved each other dearly. Dad Albert had died first with a heart attack, and twelve months later her mum Celia followed, as it was almost impossible for her to carry on. She had just seemed to fade away, yet one thing was certain: Patricia had always felt loved. They had given themselves to her and supported her throughout everything. She loved and missed them greatly.

Everything her mum and dad owned had been left to Patricia. Most of the boxes with personal belongings hadn't been sorted through. Now, for some reason, Patricia needed to do that. She spent the day in the loft going through the boxes until she found one that had a heart on it. As she pulled the tape that held it together, she saw her name - Patricia - beneath it.

Downstairs in the new kitchen, she set the box on the countertop. She had briefly been through most of the stuff in the boxes but had never before had questions that needed answering.
She filtered through the documents in the box, mostly old birth certificates, marriage certificates, letters. She wasn't sure what she was looking for, then she found a brown sealed envelope. It had her name on it.

She felt nervous and excited all at once. As she opened the envelope, she could smell perfume, not an expensive one, but one that took her back to yesterday. Inside the envelope, she found a letter from her mother.
She read it out.

Dear Patricia,

Me and your dad always loved you and always will, but we have never been able to tell you that we adopted you.
We couldn't bring ourselves to say it. Maybe we should have, but as time went by, it seemed harder and harder, especially when you couldn't have children.
You know what it's like, wanting to have children, that's why we tried to adopt legally, but we wanted a baby not a child, so, we were excited when we found Mr. and Mrs. Fisk purely by accident.
Mr. Fisk was doing some work on our house. Your dad got talking to Mr. Fisk and mentioned we had been trying for years to have a baby. It was strange because he rang us on the phone and asked if we could

meet and talk. Then he and his wife came to see us and asked us if we would like to have his daughter's baby. She was only fourteen, and we'd have to keep it quiet. Of course, we said yes! Then we made the agreement. We got your birth certificate, as your dad had a friend who just happened to know how to forge it. We had to do it because we worried you might be taken away from us.

At the time we feared we might get into trouble if anyone found out, but when you were brought to us, we were happy, so happy.

All I can say is how much we loved and love you and hope you can forgive us for not telling you.

Your loving mum and dad. xxxxxxx

At this point, Patricia could feel her body crumbling inside.
She reached inside the envelope and pulled out a small, embroidered handkerchief with the fancy letters L F with small pink and blue flowers in the corner, wrapped inside the handkerchief was a note.

Dear?

Please look after my beautiful baby. I've only known her for a few days, but I love her so much. Please call her Patricia, because I love the name, also it reminds me of someone who came into my life for a very short time and gave me hope.

Please love her as much as I do. Xxxx

Needless to say, Patricia now was in pieces and cried like never before.

A few months later, Patricia got into her car, along with Scat, and made her way to Hereford. They were going to a public house, where she had a meeting. She had been on the internet, finding her true blood relatives.
She had got in touch with her step twin sisters, aunts and uncles: her mother having passed away, her father was never known.
She had found that she had a large extended family and was hap-

pier than she could remember.

In a few quiet moments, before she left to go to see them, she stood in her old house, in the hall, looked in the long mirror and shared a few words of love with Len, who, as usual, gently encouraged her. She reflected on it all, how everything had happened: the phone box, the voice. Most people would think it was some crazy dream, that she was definitely out of her mind, but, on the wall, she had a framed picture of herself, holding a baby that was her.

How that was possible? Of course, that would be ridiculous and far too much for anyone to understand.

So, it was a secret between her and Len .... and, of course, Scat!

QUIRK-KEYS

Some city, sometime, somewhere.

"Where the hell have I put them? I can't find them anywhere!"
Tracy's growing more and more angry, more with herself, rather than with anyone else, especially as she's alone. Tracy is single, her house tidy, her mind scatty, her heart in the right place. She stands in the living room of her mid-terrace house, almost wanting to scream.

To be fair, she is a bit worse for wear, having been on the beer the night before, with a few friends from work. She has a part-time job as a dinner lady at the local primary. She has no kids of her own, but does have a boyfriend who's sometimes present, but when he isn't she doesn't rest on her laurels. Tracy likes to enjoy herself.

You could say she's a bit of a lioness; she has a fierce temper. Being short on stature, and also very slim, you wouldn't think she could bite, but she can. Then it comes to her.

"Is it possible I dropped them as I opened the door, after the taxi left?"

She makes her way to the front door.

Meanwhile, a dark shadow is gliding across the rooftops. It's a fine and beautiful day, the weather forecast having said there would be a blue sky from morning till night.

The shadow is that of a jackdaw. He swoops low and perches on the gable end of a building, his head moving from side to side, eyeing up potential breakfasts, but something else catches his curious eyes.

He looks down on the street of terraced houses where nothing is moving. This is perfect; being of a nervous disposition, things needed to be quiet.
He flies down and sees two shiny objects lying against a door. There's nothing like shiny things to a jackdaw; he's curious, cautious and capable of stealing stuff.
A bright red front door creaks slowly as it opens. Seconds later, the jackdaw is away, with two keys on a ring in his beak.

Tracy looks around outside, but can't see the keys. Now positively incandescent, she's late for work and has no choice but to go, knowing she has no way to get back in, unless her mum might have a spare set.

The jackdaw, however, flies back to his nest, with the prize in his beak. He lands just as his partner is leaving, places the shiny keys at the side of his chicks, where other small shiny things are lodged, then becomes irritated by his offspring in their need to be fed, so he flies off again to find food.

The chicks peck each other with frustration and shuffle around in the nest. In the thick of it, some of the shiny things are dislodged and they fall to the ground. In fact, they fall a fair distance and hit a middle-aged man as he's jogging by.
Kitted out in sporty Lycra, the man is a keen runner, but he's still trying to lose his beer belly which is being very stubborn and doesn't want to leave. Apart from that, and the fact he has

little hair on his head, he thinks he's pretty fit.

He feels the impact of the keys on his head. They draw a small amount of blood. He calls out,
"What the f...?"
He is breathing very heavily and is actually quite glad to have the break. The keys now lying on the ground catch his eye; he bends and picks them up, stands erect and looks up into the sky. The sun is edging up higher, he breathes in the warm air. Looking up, he can't see clearly where the keys might have come from, but he thinks it's damn strange. He raises his hand over his eyes to look up again, but to no avail.

He decides to put them in his bum bag, strapped around his waist, thinks nothing more of it and carries on running.
When he gets home, he puts the keys in a bowl on the kitchen worktop where other keys are kept. He stands at the kitchen sink, drinking copious amounts of water. He's hot, he feels good, but his mind wanders. He's a single parent now, his wife having left him for a younger model, so, what with work, home, his two growing kids, he now has his hands full. He stares blankly into the garden, then thinks, "When do I get the time for *me* in all this?"

At that moment, his daughter walks into the kitchen, dragging her school bag along the floor. She's thirteen, and late. Her dad turns around. As he does, she looks to the ground, then looks up with her so sorry-for-me eyes, then pleads for a lift to school. Like most teenagers, she's good at emotional blackmail.
He says,
"Jenny, you'll be late!"
A look of contempt is shot his way, and she groans,
"Daaad."
He zips his lips then turns towards the kitchen window to look out.

Jenny dips her hand into the key bowl, without looking, slowly walks to the front door then, as soon as she is outside, she runs like there's no tomorrow to the bus stop. She makes it; she hates it when her dad is right. She's got long blond hair, she's small for her age, and is very strong-minded. She misses her mum and resents her for breaking up the family.

Jenny is at a rebellious stage, but she's in love as well. She's applied mascara and lipstick this morning, but not enough to make a teacher send her home. She's pretty, even though here and there she has spots. She sits at the back of the bus with her friends, chats with them about Big Brother on TV, pop groups and boys. Twenty minutes later, they all get off the bus, but she dawdles behind.

The young boy from school she's in love with accidentally catches her bag as he goes by, resulting in things falling to the ground. She turns bright pink and totally speechless. He helps her pick her things up, but, in the confusion, the keys are left behind, as they have dropped into some weeds that are popping up here and there through the paving stones.

The encounter makes her day, especially as she stares into his dark brown beautiful eyes, and he says,
"It's Jenny, isn't it?"
She nods, feeling her face flush once again. The boy smiles at her then carries on his way to school. As he slowly walks away, she says,
"Thank you Robin."
But he can't hear her, so she runs after him like a lapdog.

An old lady with a stoop is walking along the footpath, hours after the kids have all gone into school. She avoids children like the plague, as they push her and call her names.
She shuffles along, her back so bent that she cannot raise her head higher than the height of her walking stick.

She is used to plodding her way to town every day. In this way, sometimes she finds things: change, notes, even jewellery.

She hoards most of it; the cash she spends on cheap whisky at the supermarket, purely medicinal, of course.

Today she stops suddenly. Seeing the shiny keys, it's like treasure to her. She rubs her hands and hums a little tune. It's a happy one, just as she is.

She's well-equipped for such occasions. In her plastic bag, there's a claw for picking up litter, which she uses to retrieve the treasure. Then she places the keys in the bag and continues to hum her way to town.

The old lady gets to the town square, finds a spot outside a big store, places a scarf on the floor, with her bag by her side. She starts to sing. People walking by look across at her and stop. They are surprised because, when she sings, she sings down to the floor, because she can't look up. Yet her voice is pure and clear and quite remarkable.

In fact, you may remember, she once came first in a talent contest on TV. She was called Florence, the Nightingale. Unfortunately, she was in a car accident, not long after she became famous, which affected her spine, so she wasn't able to continue in her quest to be a star, but she still loves to sing in public.

So, this little old lady is singing away, and the sound resonates around the square. Passers-by contribute to the monies on her scarf, commenting on how beautifully she sings. She sings without a break, mostly songs from the fifties and sixties.

As the crowd gets bigger, some people join in with the songs, and it's not long before her scarf is covered with money. Behind the crowd, four young thugs make their way towards her. They have their eyes on the cash that's lying on the scarf.

They grab the scarf with the money, along with the bag, but she's no stranger to idiots like this. She flashes her walking stick this way and that way, physically hurting two of the boys, and the scarf and money drop. A few of the onlookers grab two of the boys, but the other two have the bag and they run off.

A young mother, pushing a pram with her baby inside, is on

the other side of the square. As they run, being so preoccupied looking back, they both tumble, trying to avoid her. They drop the bag, then, fearing being arrested, at the sight of a police car which just happens to turn up, they run off, leaving it behind.

The police car immediately follows the boys, who are now running down the high street.
The young mother shushes her baby, who is now crying with all the commotion. As the baby is comforted, she picks up the Asda bag, opens it and finds the keys and the little pick-up claw. She looks at them, then is confused as to who they belong to.
The old lady has been escorted from the square by several people, consoling her on her experience, whilst the other boys have escaped as well, with nothing.
The young woman with her baby has an appointment at her doctor's, as her baby has been sleeping badly, keeping her and her husband awake. She is pressed for time, so she places the keys in the bottom of the pushchair, and continues walking through the town.

She gets to the bus stop to go to the doctors', folds the pushchair, mounts her baby on her hip in the time-honoured way, slides the pushchair in the space provided on the bus and sits for the ten minute journey.
The baby draws smiles from all around her, as the bus is quite full; so much so, the girl nearly misses her stop. She rushes down the bus, shouts to the driver to stop, grabs her pushchair then alights from the bus.
Unbeknown to her, the keys fall as the folding doors close, but a young man, sitting near the front of the bus, sees the keys, immediately gets up from his seat, picks them up, then asks the driver to stop the bus. He jumps off the bus, which then moves off. He looks up and down the road, but he can't see the young woman. Then he realises that he needs to get to work and it's too late to find the girl now and he's three bus stops short!
He clips the young woman's keys to a loop on his trousers, not

even thinking how he might get them back to her, then quickly starts running to get to work on time.

As he jogs, he looks at the green trees, the only things that brighten the area, as coke cans and cigarette ends lie in the grass, with old council houses looking seedy and unmaintained. He passes by, row after row. Here and there, a brightly-painted door stands out, along with a pretty garden and a painted fence, but mostly it's sad and depressing.

The young man is wearing a festival hoodie, with bands emblazoned on the back, which is up over his self-bleached, peaky-blinder haircut.
His thoughts get lost in a dark story of a boy who lost his way then found the key that let him unlock the princess's heart.
He saw himself as the hero: he would rescue the girl who was alone, abused and wanting a stranger to love her, and he knew he could protect her, hold on tight to her and never let her go.
Of course, she would see him as her champion.
He sees himself as a writer of sorts; where he can, he lets his imagination run wild.

The young man opens the door to Peppers Pizza Parlour, Hot and Tasty Pizzas. To Your Door. The logo is everywhere, inside and outside the shop. Gino, the owner of the shop, is making pizzas to go. Kris is one of his delivery boys and he's certain that Gino never goes home.
"Kris," he says. "Good to see you! Five pizzas to go now."
Kris scoops up the pizzas into a hot bag, steps outside the shop, stands astride his steed (mountain bike). There are no mountains, but it's great for dodging the traffic.

Kris would write most of his short stories in his head; on paper, it took too long. He'd written some stuff on his iPad, but it always sounded better in his head.

He imagines himself again, this time astride a beautiful black horse, his sword by his side, on his way to save the mysterious girl, who has been whisked away in the night by marauding pirates who were pillaging the countryside and taking away all the beautiful young girls. He feels pleased as he embellishes the words in his head.

Kris is a strong lad and speeds along on the bike. A block of flats looms ahead, six floors high, like a gloomy castle, inviting him to save everyone from the evil pirates' lair.

His mood is lifted by his story, but then he opens the door to the flats to find the lift out of order. He doesn't trust them anyway. Once before, he'd got stuck in it, with a guy and a staffy bull terrier. Kris'd had a pepperoni pizza to deliver, the dog looked like he would eat Kris and the pizza. Despite his owner saying that he wouldn't hurt a fly, Kris thought, how about a human being? Kris locks his bike in the entrance, then makes his way up the stairs.

Kris reaches the sixth floor. He's hot and bothered and breathing heavily. There's an open veranda to all the flats; he eventually gets to the last flat and knocks on the door.

Two teenagers open the door, stuff some cash in his hand and say, in unison,

"Keep the change!"

The pizza costs £14.99. The tip is a penny.

"Thanks," he says, "for nothing!"

The door slams in his face.

This is why Kris gets lost in his own fictitious world.

"People," he says to himself, "are shite, specially teenagers."

Kris has only just turned twenty.

As he walks back to the stairs, he hears a dog bark behind him. He looks round and could swear it's the same dog he encountered before in the lift, though, this time not on a lead, and without its owner. He runs like hell, crashing into a pedal bike parked outside someone's flat. He falls, ending up sprawled across the floor, then gets up quickly, leaves the bike across the walkway and careers down the stairs, never looking back once.

Kris doesn't know this, but the loop of his trousers got ripped, the keys have become dislodged and now hang on the bike's handbrake.

Early the next morning, an old guy in his sixties pokes his head out of his flat door and sees his bike lying across the walkway. He picks it up and curses,
"Fucking kids, teenagers!"
He slips back into the flat, grabs his lunchbox and hears his wife call.
"Alfie, don't forget to pick up my medication on the way home!"
Dutifully he says, "Yes love." He then heaves a rucksack over his shoulders, closes the front door, undoes the lock on his bike then makes his way downstairs, carrying the bike over the other shoulder.
It's dark, it's quiet, it's half past seven in the morning; he likes it this way. He switches on the bike lamps, mounts the bike and starts to pedal. He lives in the suburbs and is making his way into town.

Some time ago, Alfie used to fancy himself as a cyclist, having competed in many cross-country competitions and winning quite a few. But one day, on a course across the hills and forests of Wales, he was going like a bomb, the wind in his face. He could smell the pine trees, as he whizzed through them, up and down, the exhilaration phenomenal; he was lost in the excitement of it all.
He was in the lead, all the other competitors eating his dust. As he went through a particularly thick set of trees, then down a very steep bit of track, suddenly a deer was in front of him. He tried to steer to one side, but there was a limit to how much space he had. The deer, then spooked, went the same way as he did.
Alfie hit it head-on. Fortunately, the deer being softer than a tree, Alfie survived. He ended up in hospital with numerous abrasions and some broken bones. Six months later, he started

to ride again, but he was never the same.

These days he does his job, looks after his sick wife and rides to work and back. Alfie's feeling old now; not long to wait till retirement. He's worked for a water and sewage company for twenty five years, but the thought of just twiddling his thumbs at home and looking after his wife, troubles him.
Most of the day, he is underground surveying and, when needed, repairing pipes underneath the town in a world he loves.

In the darkness, Alfie brakes hard, as a car pulls up in front of him, despite most of his journey being pavement and bike lanes. The darkness early in the morning made it difficult, but in the summer usually it's stress free.

Alfie stops then notices the keys on his brake handle. He stands at the side of the road and looks at them.
"For the love of Mike," he says to himself, "Whose are these?" He thinks, but nothing comes to him. He just knows they aren't his or his wife's. He slips them into his jacket pocket, thinking he'll sort it out later.

When Alfie gets to work, he leaves his bike in a lock-up. He walks into the entrance of the grand Victorian building that is The Waterworks Company. The building always impresses him, red brick arches and pillars that today would cost millions to replicate, green ornate tiles adorning the walls, the palatial entrance welcoming. The grand Victorian building is a credit to its architects and builders.

He goes down some of the marbled stairs that can take four people abreast, into the staff room and canteen, where three men and two women are sat.
Alfie takes off his jacket, hangs it up, then sits down, after making himself a coffee. The usual mixture of chat is exchanged between the six people - TV, politics - for half an hour an enjoyable rant is taking place.

This being a change of shifts, three on, three off, Alfie and his co-workers get dressed in overalls and boots, whilst the three others make moves to get their coats and leave for home. Being distracted by the banter between them all, one of them, Arnav, picks up Alfie's jacket by mistake. Well, they are very similar in colour and design, and Alfie must have placed his coat on the wrong hook. He then leaves the building with the other workers. When he gets to his car, Arnav reaches into his hold-all, pulls out his keys, gets into his car and drives away.

By now, the city traffic has picked up, so Arnav's trip home is slow and he thinks it might be good to call in at the local supermarket to buy his wife some flowers, and maybe even some chocolates.

Arnav's feeling amorous; a night down in the dark tunnels seems to do this to him. He's not so certain his wife would feel the same, though. Arnav's got great intentions, walking round the supermarket, going even further, buying a meal for two with Prosecco thrown in.

He waits in the queue. It's still early. Arnav is a good-looking guy, thin, tall, well-proportioned, with olive skin, almost like a Mediterranean Casanova. As it becomes his turn, the girl on the till catches his eye, and says, as she's putting his things through, "Someone's going to be lucky tonight!"

Arnav feels flushed and, more than that, excited by the interaction, not that he doesn't love his wife. He stutters and smiles, saying that it could be true. There's a kind of knowledgeable look in their eyes as they chat, and, as he walks away, Arnav somehow feels taller and definitely happier.

As he leaves the supermarket, Arnav takes off his jacket, feeling hot after the short conversation. He walks to his car, reaches into his trouser pocket, takes out his mobile phone and starts to text his wife, and then hears the low growl of a motorbike behind him. He stops and moves to one side, just in case he's in the way.

Before he knows what's happening, two people on the motorbike are at his side. They wrench his jacket from him and his mobile phone, then they ride off just as quick. He runs after them, swearing, but to no avail, they're gone. He checks his pockets. Phew, he still has his wallet. All the thieves have got away with is Alfie's jacket, and, of course the keys he has no knowledge of. The two people with the black motorbike, dressed in black leathers, are now laughing to themselves as they pull up out of town.

The two riders are brothers, known as the two T's, Tom and Terry Tucker, a greasy, nasty pair, short in stature, even shorter in mentality, mean and pretty stupid. Somehow, these two villains, up to now, have evaded the law by sheer luck.

Having pocketed two phones and a handbag on their early morning thieving spree, plus of course the jacket, they've now parked up outside the home of the local fence, a dealer, a guy who lives off their ill-gotten gains.

They get to the front door of a seedy-looking semi on the shit side of town, the front garden full of car wrecks and fridges.

They make a coded knock on the window; a small fat guy appears in a dirty vest.

"Hi Vince!" they say to him.

"Hello boys! Come on in! What you got for me today?"

Inside, the Tucker brothers argue for a better price for the mobile phones and the contents of the bag. Needless to say, they're not happy.

"And as far as the jacket is concerned, it's just rubbish, the keys are useless to anyone, unless you know the door they fit," says Vince.

The Tucker brothers leave, annoyed, with a hundred quid plus the old jacket and a set of keys.

They clamber on their bike and drive off to do more thieving, unaware that, as they go, they are being followed by an unmarked car.

They make their way to the shopping centre, still being shadowed by the car. They target people on their way. Within a few miles, they grab a couple of mobile phones from unsuspecting people in the street, then zoom off, closely followed by the unmarked car. Within seconds, a police bike is on their tail; down through the town, the police follow them.

One of the brothers, when he realises they are being followed by the law, gestures to the other to get rid of the mobile phones, which he does, throwing them to the side of the road. As they narrowly avoid another police car, coming in the other direction, he then slings the coat high into the air. It floats on the breeze.

A homeless man is slumped across his old shopping-trolley full of plastic bags, cardboard and all his worldly goods; unkempt with a scruffy, long, shaggy beard, he appears somewhat bleary-eyed. He's minding his own business, occasionally sipping some strong-brew beer from a can, when the coat hits him in the face. He pulls it off his head, holds it up in front of himself, muttering, "Not bad."
He then looks up at the sky and says, "Thank you!" then crosses his chest with his finger.

He takes off a seedy old coat he is wearing, slides the new one on and says,
"Perfect!"
He slips his hands into the leather pockets, feels the keys sitting there, pulls them out and stares at them, one eye closed, to get a better focus. He chuckles to himself and burps, almost in unison, saying, in a slightly drunken manner,
"A house too!"

Meanwhile, further down the road, The Tucker Brothers have crashed head-on into a bollard, the unmarked police car having pushed them off the road. From now on, they will be needing a hospital to fix them, before they get put away with a prison sentence.

The homeless man leans against a wall, content at his good fortune, though not sure where the house might be that will fit the keys. He pushes his worldly goods around the streets in the search of it. As he meanders down the back streets, the constant squeak of his shopping trolley tells the world: Jock is coming down the street.
Halfway down he comes across a fellow homeless guy, dressed in a similar way. Obviously, they know each other and trade in friendly insults.

"Heyyy Jock! Where'd you get the new threads?"
"Aaghh, it was from heaven, Willie, just fell on me along wi' these keys inside the pocket."
Jock jangles the keys in front of Willie.
"Where's the house then, Jock?"
Jock slurs out a reply "That's what I've been looking for."
Willie laughs,
"Are you drunk before lunchtime, you silly scotch bastard? Somebody must have just lost them, with the jacket."
"What do you know about it?" replies Jock.
Willie waits a few seconds, then says,
"There's no such thing as a free lunch, unless you're like us and you find one in a waste bin!"
With this, a broad smile climbs across both their faces.
"Anyway, I'm a betting man. Jock, your chances of finding that house are millions to one. I mean," Willie says, with his right fingerless glove pointing, "Seeee, Jock! There's no chance in hell they would fit that red door."
Willie passes the keys back to Jock, who eyes the door and holds the key to his right eye, then stretches it out at arm's length, almost as if to see if it will fit at three meters away.
Jock shakes his head.
"You're right, Willie, millions to one."
Jock then looks at Willie as he reaches into his shopping trolley.

"Do you fancy a wee drink, Willie?"
An almost unintelligible reply comes out of Willie's mouth.
" Oiiihie, lead on Mcduff!"
As they stagger on, Jock tosses the keys into the kerb.
A few minutes later, in the distance, you can hear them singing
"Donald where's yer troozers?"… almost in harmony.

Soon afterwards, a battered ten-year-old blue Peugeot pulls up in front of the house with the red door. Out gets Tracy, who had decided to stay at her mum's overnight, having not found her keys. She's still muttering to herself about her bloody keys, as she waits for her mum to get out of the driver's side of her car.

Tracy is still slowly seething, as she has had to listen to her mum lecturing her on her drinking habits, waywardness and just … being.

Like all good mothers, Tracy's mum wants the best for her daughter. As she gets out of the car, she brings up the subject of grandkids. At this, Tracy, now visibly agitated, waits by the door and does her best to change the subject. But, as her mum comes round the car, she bends down and says,
"What's this, then?"
As she rises, like a phoenix from the ashes, she holds up two shiny keys and jangles them at Tracy.
"What the f…?", says Tracy. "So, they were there all the time?"
"Looks like it." her mum says. "You're bloody lucky nobody ever broke into your house!"

They stand together, outside the door. Tracy slides the key in the door and they go inside.

CRAZY FACE

William woke up, pushed his feet out of bed and surveyed his room. He put his hands to the side of the bed and pushed himself gingerly up, slipped on his dressing gown, then made his way downstairs. He went into the kitchen, sat down on a stool, placed some white bread in the toaster. From where he sat, he could reach everything. This was the nice thing about having a small kitchen; all the necessary things were on the table - butter, milk, knife, spoon, cup, saucer, plate.

William's mind wasn't military, but he liked order. The toaster popped, so he reached across and placed the toast on the plate. He buttered the toast, having already poured the tea, then, with a satisfying crunch, he slowly ate the toast, following each mouthful up with a sip of the hot sugared tea.

Despite his home being a small space, it was enough for William. He was content in here; it was safe and homely. The sun was shooting rays across the kitchen whilst vapour from the kettle was sliding up the wall, alongside the shadow of his face. He watched it on the wall. It was larger than life and made him look like a monster, but he was used to it.

William lived in a terraced house, two up two down. Most of the houses had been altered in his street to allow for an upstairs bathroom, but William had left his bathroom downstairs, next to the kitchen. His mother used to say, "It fits its purposes." William thought the same and he stuck to it. The house itself was nicely decorated, although the furniture had seen better days. William was not one for change.

William was a bulky man, but not fat. In his early thirties, his demeanour on a good day was good, but on a bad day, he was slow. He suffered with a limp and used a stick to walk. Usually, the weather was a big factor; cold and damp he didn't like but if it was a nice day, William was happier about everything,

After breakfast William prepared himself to leave. He stopped and looked in the hall mirror, the only mirror in the house. He stared for a few minutes at the reflection of his face and, seeing nothing that needed attention, he took a sharp intake of breath, turned to the door and made his way outside.
There was a small garden at the front. He looked down, saw rubbish everywhere as a dustbin had rolled over. Kids probably, or a fox. He sat the bin upright and pushed some of the rubbish back in the bin. He couldn't sort it all out now; that would mean going back in the house, getting gloves and more bags, so he left it.
He moved toward the gate, held the catch, but before he opened it, he looked up and down the street. His heartbeat became faster. As he took in all he could see, he thought how ugly it all was, in comparison to how beautiful it was inside his home.
He went out of the gate. Today, he had left his stick behind, as the weather was fine. Many cars were parked down the street, which looked dirty: dog mess, litter, cigarettes.

It was autumn, so William was wearing a big coat and a hat. This time of year, he always felt more comfortable, as he could hide under warm clothing. He only had a short walk to the bus stop, yet this was when he felt most vulnerable. He was lost in his thoughts when, suddenly, a dog stuck its nose out through a gate, as William was walking past, and immediately started to bark crazily. This unnerved him; he pulled his collar up closer round his face, continued onto the main road for a few hundred yards and was soon waiting for a bus.

William worked for the council in a small office. It was mainly computer work, all to do with refuse collection. There was never a time that William was to the front of anything; you would always find him at the back, in the shadow, away from acknowledgement. He felt comfortable that way, so when there was a queue he would be at the back.

The bus was full; he nearly didn't get on. There were a few seats but not at the back, where he preferred. Today, the only free seats were side seats. He hated these, as it would mean occasionally having to look at the opposite person or people.

He sat and immediately looked away or down. The journey was twenty-five minutes, so not the end of the world, but uncomfortable. Towards the end of the journey, the bus jerked. Everybody moved back then forward in an alarming fashion. Some people laughed, whilst others complained. Yet the driver was unmoved.

A few people got off, a few got on.

William allowed his eyes to be lifted from the floor. There was now someone else seated opposite him. He saw beautiful sky-blue eyes staring at him. She too had a scarf high above the neck and a hat. After all, it was a cold day. He quickly looked round at others on the bus, but there was nothing unusual, as everyone was wrapped up warm. This woman, however, was different. Those eyes drilled into his thoughts.

Far too quickly, he was at his bus stop and he had to get off. He wanted so much to speak, but before he knew it, he was standing by the side of the road.

The day followed its usual pattern; whilst he went through the motions, in the back of his head those eyes troubled him. He caught the bus home and wondered if he would ever see the woman with beautiful blue eyes again, and if he didn't, he knew that that thought would darken his evening.

As he walked up his street, it was bathed in lamplight. In the semi-darkness, he never felt vulnerable, as the shadows suited him. Once home, going through the door, the womb would take over; he would feel safe. But it was Friday, so he felt even safer. On the way home, he bought a few essentials, as he tended to do a big shop once a month, filling his fridge and freezer, then small things during the week.

That night, he reflected on his brief encounter; how could he think of it though? Other than eyes just connecting in a public place, it didn't mean anything. He slept badly, woke up several times thinking about her, yet his dreams were not full of the usual stranger things.

William got up early the next morning and sat in the kitchen, following his usual breakfast routine. This calmed him and allowed him to feel himself again. After breakfast, he did some washing and cleaned around the house, whilst still in his pyjamas; he loved the informality of it. He then had a shower, got dressed, went downstairs and looked in the mirror.
William stared at his reflection and his mind backtracked. Sometimes he felt mental pain and stress because of his appearance, but nothing like that he had experienced during his school days, which inevitably resulted in his mother being called in. He would stand up to it all very well, shedding a few tears, yet inside, he was always screaming out for peace.
After all, he had been like this since he was a baby, but for now, William's world was here; not back then, he hated back then. Now he was in control, at least in his own house he was.

William moved towards the back door. The sun was coming

through the window once again and the cold air took his breath away, as he opened the door. He stepped into the garden where there was a small lawn, some plants in pots and a path which cut a line down the centre of the lawn. A six-foot fence surrounded the garden, at the end of which stood a shed - his shed, his castle, his second home, and his most favourite place on Earth. He remembered saying that to his mother. The shed had been built by his dad, many years ago.

His father left his mother when William was small, yet his mother never talked about it. William never wanted to worry his mother by asking about his father; she always looked after him, so he never needed a dad.

The shed had an all-glass front to it so there was plenty of light. William walked up to the side, unlocked the door and stepped inside, where there was a desk with a swivel chair in front of it. Some notes, blank paper and a pot of dry flowers sat on the desk; around the walls there were words and little drawings.

William leant down below the desk, turned on the table lamp and the heater, then rubbed his hands together and breathed out the vapour that was visible in the cold air. William loved to write and draw more than anything in the world. Now he felt content. It didn't take long before the shed was warm. William sat at a laptop and started to tap out a story, and every now and again, he would make a tiny sketch of what was in his mind.

Angel's Bridge by William Norse.

The water was running slow and cold, the shadows were long and dark, the bridge was foreboding. From beneath, the light bounced up and down on the water like shards of glass; here and there you could hear water dripping from the underside of the bridge, like an uneven tune. The bricks looked sad; with angled shapes and high-water marks, it made it an eery place to be in. Down in the water, it was a dead, dark colour.

The bridge, which spanned the small river, had a high arch, each end of which sank into the water, so, from the bank, it looked like a dark, lonely moon, sitting half in, half out of the water. It served to connect the villages and towns and, unusually, it was very wide, so wagons could pass on it. Placed as it was in the countryside on the edge of a village, it had a tale to tell but nobody wanted to talk, so it sat and waited.

Angel had finished all her chores and was walking over the bridge. As she crossed, she looked down at the water; it looked cool. Today had been very hot, and down there on the bank she could see it was nice and shallow and there was a sandy beach.

Angel made her way down. The bank was steep, so this wasn't easy, but when she got there, she placed her feet in the cooling water and sat on the sand. As she washed her hands and face, she saw her reflection. She was beautiful. If she wasn't a mere farmer's daughter, you would have said she was a princess. A warm smile crossed her face. She felt good to be in her skin, she now felt refreshed. Her eyes were drawn to the water, especially directly under the bridge. In the middle of the river, the water was perfectly still, yet the water at the edges ran fast; where it was still, the water seemed to glow with many colours, and she seemed transfixed by it.

Angel sat there for an hour, not being able to move, then she heard a voice. It was her sister, calling from above on the bridge.
"Father needs you to help with the cows."
Angel, aged 17, had three younger sisters. As she snapped out of her trance, her sister went home. Angel stood there, her feet still in the water. She went to lift them out so she could dry them on the warm grass, but she could not move them. She was stuck. She looked down to see hundreds of tiny fish around her feet and, as she tried harder to take her feet out, she felt herself move in the water. It appeared as if the tiny fish were carrying her further into the river.

The sight of this young, beautiful girl being carried by hundreds of fish was something to behold. She looked as if she was standing on the water and slowly moving towards the arch of the bridge. Angel laughed as the fish bore her off to the middle of the river and she neared the ever-changing colours in the water. The fish dived deeper, taking her down. Now she panicked. She could not swim! She called for help, but none was there. In a few moments, Angel was gone.

Angel awoke on the grassy bank, sat up quickly and saw the bridge. She heard birds singing overhead; for a moment, it seemed a dream had taken her, but she was soaked and, now feeling cold, she got to her feet and ran quickly back to her home.

Days passed, even weeks, yet Angel still thought about that day, wondering whether it may have just been a dream. As the certainty that it was real became stronger, so did the increasing sense of euphoria, every time she thought of it.

She talked about the bridge to her mother and father and asked them why people went quiet whenever it was mentioned. Her parents passed a concerned look to each other and said,
"Stay clear of the river by the bridge! It is dangerous! That's all!"
This said, Angel never spoke about it again.

However, Angel was curious and felt no fear, so before long she found time and went back. There was a cool wind, so the water was choppy and, as before, in the middle of the river, under the arch, the water was calm and changing into many colours. Once more, Angel lay her feet in the water and, as she stood, she was swept away by the small fish. Again, she laughed and, as she got closer to the calm water, she slowly went down.

At that moment, a man on a dark horse was passing over the bridge. He looked down and saw the beautiful girl, drowning in the water. She looked up at the man, dressed in black; he looked down, exchanging glances for a few moments. But she was going down! She screamed.

Angel awoke, as before, on the grass by the river. This time, the handsome stranger was looking into her eyes.

"How are you?" he asked but his voice left her speechless. He continued. "I understand. You must have been terrified."

Angel thought for a moment and realised she had not been scared at all. He picked her up and carried her up the bank, as if she were a feather. They both looked at each other.
"Where do you live?" he asked.
She pointed towards a small group of houses further down the road. From the bridge he carried her there, his horse dutifully following, not far behind.
At the little farmhouse, there was much going on. As he approached, the three sisters ran towards him, as did Angel's parents. Within a short time, Angel was in bed and the handsome man was on his way.

The next day, Angel made her way downstairs and, as she sat to eat breakfast, they all stared. Her father said, "What did I tell you about the river?"
Angel was quiet. She didn't feel it necessary to speak, but now her head was not only hypnotised by the river but also by the handsome man.

Angel spoke, "What was the man's name?"
Her three sisters smiled in unison, but it was her father who replied. "Strangely, he said his name was Samuel Black. He had a black horse and from head to toe, he was dressed in black. He told me he was a merchant who travelled the roads, selling his wares in the towns and cities."
Angel looked down and her sisters giggled. Angel threw them a withering look, but they continued to giggle. Their father became impatient, stood up and left the room. As he was leaving, he turned and spoke to Angel.
"We have much work to catch up on Angel, so hurry up!"
Angel grabbed some bread and followed her father out.

It wasn't long before Samuel Black was back; three days to be precise. Soon it would be regular visits to see Angel. A few months passed and there was talk of marriage. One day, as he was riding to see her, he spotted her by the river. He got off his horse and walked down to where she was.

"This is where we first met," he said.

If truth be told, Angel came here every day to stare at the river. Samuel got down on one knee, looked up at the beautiful Angel and said,

"Will you marry me?"

With great joy, she replied,

"Yes of course I will!" but then added, "Wash your feet with me!"

Samuel took off his boots and sat next to Angel. As the cool waters passed over their feet, Angel said,

"Look at the water!"

Samuel looked out into the river and, right beneath the bridge, the water was flat calm with multicolours dancing on its surface. They were both mesmerised by it.

Angel stood up, as did Samuel. She held his hand. Thousands of tiny fish bore them away to the centre of the river. Angel said nothing but Samuel was confused and asked,

"What is this?"

He looked down as they travelled out into the river. He observed Angel, noticing her air of calmness and, with the look of love in their eyes, they embraced and kissed. Then the river slowly took Angel and Samuel to its depths.

Samuel's horse was found whinnying and scraping at the ground near the water's edge, yet Angel and Samuel's bodies were never found.

Many people believed that Angel was a witch and that it was she who had stolen away Samuel's life, but who are we to say? When it comes down to love, surely, we are all bewitched?

Angel's Bridge
A plaque on the bridge

Here true love was found and forever lost
It is thought that these waters were cursed
By witches who were drowned in the river

By a ducking stool in 1780

William finished the story, feeling happy that in death there was true love. It's better than none at all. If only he could know true love.

It was dark when he went back into the house. The central heating was on, so the house was warm. William ran himself a bath, the routine of the weekend slipped by, and, as Sunday evening approached, the trepidation of Monday also brought about the hope he may see again the woman with the beautiful eyes.

Monday morning.
William was in his kitchen. As he was eating his breakfast, the sun made its way again across the kitchen. Another day without my stick, he thought. On leaving, he never looked in the mirror. "This could be a first!"
He turned at the gate, looked down the street, then started to walk to the bus stop.

Then it happened.

That dread inside him hit him. He heard the voice, calling to him,
"Hey, crazy face! Where you been hiding that ugly mug?"

William kept his head down and decided to walk quicker, but this hurt his legs. He managed only one pace before the voice taunted him once more. William never responded, but the teenager rode past on his bike, continuing to throw words of hatred at him. He reached the bus stop; thankfully, the boy had gone.
On the bus, William got to the back seats and slid to the end, where he relaxed. The bus wasn't as full today. As the stops went by, he looked up and across. On the other side of the bus, in the respective corner, there she was. She looked towards him; he caught her eyes. Now he could see more of her face and she caught some of his. He smiled; she smiled; his heart danced.

He was reaching his stop, so he slid out of the seat, leant across and said,

"Hi! I'm William! How are you? I've never seen you on the bus before!"

He was shocked by his braveness, but he knew time waits for no-one. She answered,

"I'm ok! My name's Alice."

She paused and nervously took a breath.

"I've just moved to the area. I work in the town."

William smiled, she smiled. He didn't know what else to say. The bus was slowing down for his stop. Without thinking, he took her hand and kissed the back of it, causing her to blush. He bowed to her and said,

"See you tomorrow!"

He made his way down the bus and then alighted, stood and waved. Alice waved back; William had a hundred Christmases all in one go.

Mondays had always been a dirge, a darkness, a mindset that William could never get to grips with, but this Monday was like the stars had given yet more light on an already sunny day. On his way home, there was almost a skip in his step that, to a man who found it sometimes difficult to walk on a bad day, was nothing short of a small miracle.

As the weeks went by, slowly but surely, William and Alice would meet each other and would go for a meal at a discrete restaurant. They even went to a pub, getting to know each other better, until one day, he asked her to come home with him. As they walked up his road, a feeling of intense dread came over William and, sure enough, the teenage boy came riding his bike down the street. The words fell out of his mouth like abusive sick, only this time he screamed as he went by.

"Oh my God! Two crazy faces!"

Immediately, William's embarrassment was tangible, but he put his arm around Alice and rushed her home. Once behind closed doors in his home, all was different. For the first time in his life, William felt normal, whatever normal was.

Late that night, a taxi took Alice home and, even though the bully had made their life hell earlier, they had both forgotten it and had enjoyed their night together.

William awoke, sat up, slipped his legs out of bed, surveyed the room, put his hands to his side and lifted himself up gingerly. He went downstairs to the small kitchen, stood at the window, ate his toast, drank some tea and said to himself,
"It's a damp day today."
He got dressed and made his way to the front door, never once looking in the mirror. He lifted his stick from the hall stand, opened the front door, then walked to the front gate. Not once did he look down the street; he saw nothing bad, felt nothing but good.

Then he heard it. The teenage yob was, yet again, giving William abuse, but something stirred in William. His mind stood up to attention and he felt hatred. William could hear the boy on his bike, not far behind him, so, just as the tirade was getting louder and the teenager was riding past on his bike, instinctively, William pushed out his stick and poked it through the spokes of the front wheel of his bike. The boy shot over the top of the handlebars, crashing headfirst on the ground.

Silence.

William stood over the boy. Blood was pouring down his face. As the boy lifted his head, William could see that he had a badly broken nose and several cuts, some quite deep, to his face. The boy swore at William,
"You bastard! You could have killed me! I'll sue you! You'll pay!"
William said,
"What have I done? You fell off your bike! What's it got to do with me?"
The boy started to cry. William leant down and said,

"What's it like to have a crazy face, you fucking hooligan?"

William and Alice went to town together, something they never ever did normally. They both had feelings which they had never had before at any time with anyone, so this was an adventure. Alice loved shoes, so they found themselves outside a shoe shop and looked in the window. All the shoes were presented with large mirrors behind them.

William saw his reflection. He looked at his face. He could see that one eye was a lot lower than the other, his nose was large for his face, his lips looked lop-sided; indeed, his face was uneasy with itself. As Alice looked at herself, she saw that almost at a forty-five-degree angle, she had a birth mark across her face, dark red in colour that went across her nose and her mouth and made her lips look larger. They caught each other's eyes and then, as they both looked down at their hands, held tightly, reflected in the mirror, they both knew it was the most beautiful sight in the world...

GHOST SHUFFLE

Darren was listening to *Here Comes the Sun,* by The Beatles, on his iPod. It shuffled all his favourite songs which were specially picked for the journey. He stood in his bedroom, looking like a latter-day hippy - long hair, seventies-looking clothes. He stared at himself in the long mirror on the wall of his bedroom, to make sure he looked ok. He was about six foot tall and well-built but by no means overweight. Looking at his reflection he said,

"Yes, you look fine."

He was better than fine; his high cheekbones, which he had inherited from his mother, gave him an almost angelic look, while his nicely trimmed full beard gave him the air of masculinity. The clothes he wore would fit in nicely in India and, to all intents and purposes, even here. He was on his way to London to meet Vanessa, his girlfriend, then together they would fly to India. Although they had only known each other a short time, they shared the same dream: to go to India for a spiritual awakening and, of course, to learn. The song filled him with optimism.

Darren's parents had met Vanessa, for the first time, a few months previously, in a pub, halfway between Worcester and Ross-on-Wye. They'd asked all the relevant questions and, even though they had their reservations, Darren's parents gave them both their blessings. Vanessa was half-Asian; her father was an actor, her mother, who came from India, a cookery writer. She was very encouraging to them both, having very liberal views about love, life, and the world as a whole.

Darren looked well-set for the adventure. He had had a regime of healthy eating and exercise and, by now, he was almost vegetarian. His mum fussed over him, making sure he had everything. As he went downstairs, his dad did the same. They'd made sure he had enough money in his bank account, so that, in any emergency, he could come home. He left the house with a tear in his eye. His mum and dad tried to hide theirs.

Darren reached the main A road going south. As he walked, he sang along to the music on his iPod. *Bright Side of The Road*, by Van Morrison, was playing. *Perfect* he thought. The weather seemed to be set fair but, suddenly, the skies turned dark grey, and it started to rain. Lightly at first, so this didn't bother him. He slipped on his trusted plastic mac with a hood which he'd used many times at festivals, when the weather turned bad. The rain got heavier. It was atrocious. He walked along the road with his thumb in the well-accepted way to gain a lift. It was in his mind to give up and find some cover till it passed over.

He was on the A49, one of the busiest roads in Herefordshire, so he thought it was just a question of time till somebody would take pity on him and give him a lift.

Just then, as he turned to look at the on-coming traffic, he could feel the rain dripping down his face. Then, all of a sudden, he felt his head spinning, as if he had been drinking too much. Not an unpleasant feeling, but enough to make everything turn into multicoloured layers.

All he could hear was the music of Crosby, Stills and Nash, *Sweet*

Judy Blue Eyes, on his iPod, his earplugs planted firmly in his ears. The harmonies seemed to calm him, as he slowly opened his eyes. He was lying on the floor in the back of a van. He had no idea how he'd got there; it took time for his mind to get to grips with the situation.

Then, suddenly, he thought, somebody *did* take sympathy on the hitchhiker in the rain. He went to pull his earplugs out, but found it impossible to move. Panic went through his mind, thinking he had been kidnapped, but he knew his mum and dad had no money.

Rationalising his thoughts, whilst trying to move some part of his body, he realised he could see and move his eyes.

Another track came on his iPod. It was another oldie, The Beatles' *Ticket to Ride.* The up-beat music helped him to focus. He concentrated on his fingers, tried to shuffle himself around, even attempted to shout, but his lips wouldn't move. He realised that trying to move his body was useless.

Then he decided to relax, be cool; maybe then he would be able to move. Concentrating again on his hands, slowly the ends of his fingers started to flex. It was working. At the same time, he was aware that the van would stop abruptly now and again, before moving off.

Darren was sliding up and down the van, with little hope of stopping himself from bashing into the back door. The van stopped again. It seemed his body was coming back to life. He was nearly able to move to a crouching position. It seemed like all his limbs were now working but, in fact, it felt like his whole body was foreign to him. He could move and feel yet felt somehow disengaged. Like the morning-after-the-night-before. He needed to find out who was driving this bloody van. Stumbling over some parcels up to a small window to the front of the van, he looked through it. He could see the driver. He bashed on the glass, tried to shout but he had no voice. The driver seemed oblivious to all this.

He stared at the driver, willing him to look around. Then an even stranger feeling made everything weirder because *All Along the Watchtower,* by Jimi Hendrix, came on his iPod.
He thought he must be in some strange dream. He had tried cannabis a couple of times, but he was a mere novice. This sensation was other-worldly. Then, he blacked out. Just before he did, he could feel pins and needles all over his body.

Darren found himself sat by the road. He rested his head between his hands as if to calm a blinding headache. He opened his eyes. Strangely It wasn't raining. He was dry. It all looked familiar. He had been here only moments earlier. This was where he'd started to hitchhike. More importantly, this was where he could remember his head starting to spin. On his iPod, *California Dreaming,* by Jose Feliciano, was playing. This eased his trauma.

His rucksack was by his side. He took off his plastic mac, folded it up and put it in the bag. In a pocket was his water bottle containing some fruit juice. He took a sip. It tasted strange; it somehow tasted of nothing. He tried to stand up. He thought it must be some out-of-body experience: maybe the weather, perhaps the excitement of leaving home. His mum and dad were behind him with his plan. They'd all thought a long holiday, specially to India, would be a good experience before college but, at that moment, he felt like he was going nowhere.

Darren couldn't manage another step, so he stayed where he was for a moment, then moved back a couple of meters, away from the road, towards some wooden fencing. His iPod was still on. He took the earplugs out and drifted off to sleep.

When he woke up, he felt different; he had no pain, he didn't feel tired, he wasn't feeling sick. In fact, he felt good. He got up, slung his bag over his shoulder and made his way along the main road again. It was pleasant. The sun was out. He felt at one with the world, but something nagged his thoughts. *I feel too good.*

The road ahead was busy. He stuck his thumb out and walked that walk that hitchhikers do, half looking back. Sometimes looking as if they might fall over at any second.

He stopped for a moment to interrupt his iPod. Being on shuffle meant you get any one of your thousands of songs. He had grown to dislike this one. He skipped it. The odd one sometimes didn't fit the moment.

Buck Rogers came on, by Feeder. One of his favourite songs.

At that moment, he saw a car had pulled in up ahead, with a door open. He picked up his pace. He went straight up to the open back door and clambered in over a child's car seat. He made himself comfortable. He then took out one earplug and said, "Thanks so much!" to the male driver.

As he looked out of the window, he noticed a woman with a small child, who seemed to be having a wee in the bushes. A few minutes later, the woman fastened the child back in the car seat. As she got back in, Darren thanked her too.

There was no response, so Darren took it that that was it, for the moment. He replaced his earplug.

They were back in the traffic, which had come to a standstill. Darren was glad to be back on the road to London, even though they weren't moving. A calming track came on his iPod. *Theme from Boat Weirdos,* by Joe Walsh. He closed his eyes and thought of Vanessa.

They'd met via Facebook. He couldn't remember how; a friend of a friend maybe. Becoming friends from then on, they had found things they liked about each other, mostly based around travelling. As time went by, they would meet somewhere be-tween Hereford and London. They liked each other immedi-ately and started to make plans to travel some day in the fu-ture to India. Darren was studying languages and broadening his horizon. Vanessa was going to university to study nutrition, helped by the fact that her mum was a qualified chef.

Darren had been questioning his decision to hitch to London for a while now. He had thought to try and start the adventure the moment he left his mum and dad's house. He was now feeling that, maybe, that had been a mistake. He opened his eyes as the car moved slowly forward.

The little boy in the child seat was about two years old and was now staring at Darren, sat next to him. Darren stuck out his tongue. The boy laughed. Darren did it again. The boy laughed more, causing his mother to look back.

"What are you laughing at, Sean?"

He carried on laughing, then said,

"Man funny!"

Darren felt disturbed by what happened next.

"What do you mean, Sean? What man, where?"

Darren stopped putting his tongue out. The boy stopped laughing. Darren said,

"I'm here! What's the matter? Can't you see me? You stopped to pick me up?"

The woman smiled at Sean and turned back to face the front window. The man asked,

"Is he ok?"

"Yes of course he is! He must be tired," she replied.

Darren felt strange. The traffic was moving again. Suddenly, the same sensation as before pulled him back to where he had been by the side of the road, less than an hour ago. Pins and needles was all he could feel.

Darren's love of music was eclectic. He had listened to all his mum and dad's records as a kid, plus many more besides and, of course, he had broadened his own taste as well. Never into rap or garage music, his thoughts were more traditional.

At that moment, The Beatles' *Within You Without you* filtered through his head. It relaxed him; he loved the sitar.

The funny thing was, he didn't feel panicked. He was easy with what was happening because he thought that, eventually, he would get where he was going.

He had been practising yoga and mindfulness, so he thought, somehow, all things were solvable. After all, life's a journey and this was part of it. The truth was, Darren sensed that there was something wrong. He was an intelligent young man, but it seemed this penny had a long way to drop.

Darren got up. A thought came to him, as he was sitting in the same spot once again. This time, he started to walk back towards home. He remembered that, just before he'd got there, there was a local bus stop, a mile back down the road. The weather was still fine, he still felt good. His iPod picked *Champagne Supernova* by Oasis. It somehow seemed appropriate. He walked meaningfully, head down, to catch a bus. He thought about his mum and dad. They'd been together for over thirty years and they had given him everything they could. They were both retired and living in the country. He couldn't help but feel homesick and he was only ten miles from home.

The traffic passed by. *How Can I Tell You* by Cat Stevens came on Darren could feel his emotions. Standing at the bus stop, a tear came into his eye. He wiped it away, as a bus pulled up next to him, then stood to one side to allow several people to get off. Once on board, he took out the still eligible pass that his mum and dad had bought for him, showed it to the driver, who didn't seem interested. Of course, Darren was already in two minds about what was happening to him. He just wanted to talk to someone, anyone.

On the single decker bus, he went to the back, where there were seats opposite each other. He sat on one. There were two girls sitting in the corner seat, chatting to each other. He looked across at them, smiled and waved half-heartedly. Nothing, no response. He got up, leaned across, stared at them and said,
"Hi! Can you see me?"
Then he heard someone speak. A man, who had just sat opposite him, said,
"They can't see you, mate! You're dead."

The shock winded Darren. He fell back into his seat.
"I'm Sid."
He patted Darren on the knee, then continued.
"It hits you hard. There's no-one to tell you. You learn it the hard way and when it's said, it's like a brick in the stomach."
Darren sat still. He was stunned. Obviously, he'd guessed something was not right. But just being told like that shocked him badly.
"I'll tell you a few things that might help," Sid added.
Darren had been sat, head down, staring at the floor. As he looked up, Sid was now lying across the two seats, smoking a cigarette. Darren realised there was no tobacco smell. He studied Sid carefully. He had very short hair at the sides and back, with a longish quiff over the top of his head. He had a sharp, pale face like a latter-day Elvis, but ten times thinner. He was wearing all black leathers and black fingerless gloves. Sid looked across at Darren, and said,
"What's on your iPod?"
Darren hesitated, still trying to process what Sid was talking about.
"Oh, tons of music, all sorts."
"Any Sex Pistols, or Punk?" asked Sid.
"No."
"So that's pretty shit then."

Darren was perplexed that this extrovert personality was talking to him and he felt that he wasn't keeping up. And now he was insulting Darren's taste in music.
Sid leaned across and pulled out Darren's ear plugs.
"It's ok. I'd turned it down," said Darren.
Sid raised both his hands in peace. Darren took a deep breath, then Sid continued.
"When I crashed my motorbike, no more than five miles from here, all I had as I sat at the side of the road was a pack of cigarettes and a lighter. I found out they never run out, but I can't taste them. Your iPod is all you have and whatever's in your

backpack. The iPod won't go flat and that bottle of water there, in the side of your backpack, won't run out either, but you'll never taste it. The truth is, you won't need to eat or drink. There's thousands of people like us."

Darren had difficulty keeping up with the rules of deadness.

He said,

"I haven't seen any apart from you."

"That's because you didn't know you were dead till now. Don't worry, one thing about us now we're dead, we can't do anyone any harm, not even to each other. We are all caught between here and whatever. At some stage, we have to let go and so do our loved ones. Until that happens, we are stuck here, but when they do let go, that's when the fading begins."

"What do you mean?" asked Darren.

"You'll find out soon enough," said Sid.

Darren replaced his earphones and turned the iPod up. The Cure came on singing *Friday I'm in love.* Darren's mind was in a quandary. The bus continued its local bus route, down country lanes in Herefordshire. Sid and Darren were silent. They watched as people got off and then on to the bus. Then, the strangest thing happened. An elderly man, in his late sixties, climbed on board the bus, shuffled up the aisle and sat next to Sid. The old man had on an old, long dressing-gown with blue and white stripes running down it. His medium-length grey beard made him look a bit like Father Christmas. He was wearing carpet slippers and on his head was perched a pink hat with rabbits' ears. His warm, kind eyes looked across at Darren, who nodded in acknowledgment. Sid patted the guy on the knee and said,

"You ok Martin?"

Martin replied,

"Yes, I'm fine."

The weirdest thing was that Martin was how you might imagine a ghost to be; you could almost see through him. Sid said to Martin,

"Tell Darren here how you died."

Martin immediately had a broad smile which lit up his face.

"It was Christmas Day. My daughter and grandchildren had come round. My youngest granddaughter, who is 3 years old, was opening presents and she stuck this hat on my head. She started to laugh at me. I made faces at her. She laughed more, so I did too and apparently, then, I had a heart attack. I died happy, but I didn't know that at the time. For a couple of days, I just hung around and watched. They had my funeral. I saw them crying, but it didn't affect me. It seems the living suffer so much when people die and yet we don't."

"How long have you been dead?" asked Darren.

"Must be nine months now, but I'm not sure," replied Martin. Darren looked across at Sid and asked,

"What does everyone do with their time?"

"Nothing," answered Sid, "No need to! While you're here you're free to wander."

"Do you sleep?"

"Yes of course!" said Martin. Sid nodded in agreement. Martin continued,

"Best sleep I've had in years! I had terrible arthritis. Couldn't sleep at all most nights. Now I sleep like a baby."

"Where do you sleep?" asked Darren. "At your home?"

"No, I don't go back there anymore. I don't like to see what I'm not part of. Anyway, I can sleep anywhere, on the floor, grass, bush, shed, bus, it doesn't matter. The cold doesn't affect us, nor the heat. It's perfect deadness."

"It looks like you're on your way," Sid said. "Looks like they're letting you go."

"Yes," said Martin. Darren then asked,

"Where do we go after this then?"

Sid and Martin looked at each other and said in unison,

"No idea."

Sid got up and gestured to Darren to follow. Just before they made their way off the bus, the two shook Martin's hand and wished him "Good luck."

He smiled.

"It's been a pleasure."

They got off the bus. Another passenger placed her baby in a pushchair. As she got off, Sid made faces at the baby. The baby cried. Darren quickly smiled and put his tongue out at the baby, who then smiled.

"I get great pleasure out of doing that," said Sid. "It's strange, but true. Only babies and small children can see us."

They were in a small village on the western edge of Herefordshire. Darren followed Sid as they walked across a field of corn that reached just above their knees.

"Where are we going?" asked Darren.

"To show you a Ley line," replied Sid.

"Why?"

"Do you know about them?"

Darren's eyes lit up and he enthusiastically replied,

"As a matter of fact, I do. My mum and dad have one running through their garden. They are lines drawn between historic and ritual sites having some sort of magnetic connection running between them."

Sid was impressed. They reached a spot at the edge of the field.

"Well," said Sid, "Here is a Ley line and one thing ghosts can't do is cross them. Something to do with the magnetic energy they create. All over the country these things crisscross and, if you die inside that area, that's where you stay till you fade."

Then he put his hand out in front of him, into some imaginary space. It disappeared, then his arm, all the way up to his shoulder. He brought it back.

"Wow!" said Darren, "That's amazing! What does it feel like?"

"It feels like pins and needles; makes you feel quite numb."

Sid kept on shaking his arm to get the circulation going. Then Darren said,

"Hang on, that's what I felt a couple of times today, when I was back at the side of the road."

He explained to Sid what had happened. Sid said,

"What you did, Darren, was go full pelt into the Ley line that sends you straight back to where you died. Only if you take your whole body through, then it sends you back."

These two mismatched men stood at the edge of that field. All that could be heard was skylarks, way up above them, singing for all they were worth. They walked back. Darren put his iPod back on. Sid took out his cigarettes, as they plodded across the field. The beat that was emanating from Darren's earplugs could be clearly heard. *You've Got a Friend,* by James Taylor.

The evening was closing in, as the sun dipped below the trees. Darren found himself with Sid in a pub beer garden. A few people were at the tables, eating and drinking. Here and there, Darren noticed others like himself and Sid. They seemed to be drawn to the sound and the ambiance: the good spirit, capturing the light and sound of life that the dead could get closer to.

Darren couldn't remember the date. He was sure it was the same day he'd set out to meet Vanessa. He couldn't quite get to grips with his feelings. It was like nothing really mattered anymore, and, of course, it didn't. He kept thinking about his mum and dad. They still might not know he was dead. He was pretty certain Vanessa wouldn't. His iPod then played *I Don't Believe in Miracles,* by Colin Blunstone. This was one of his mum and dad's favourites. If he could have, he would have, but the tears wouldn't come.

Then, as if from nowhere, he heard an accordion, a drum and a violin. It was eerie. It filtered up through the streets. He got up and started to walk towards it. All the other spirits followed.

They walked through the village. More and more spirits joined them. The sun was setting on a hill, way in the distance, the light magical, the air still, a slight mist hanging over the distant trees. The sound of music was out of this world.

The spirits turned into a field, on which a dozen Morris dancers, dressed in coats made of strips of multicoloured material, their faces blacked up, were dancing back and forth, almost as if in slow motion. As they beat their sticks in time, they turned and twisted, their coats all of a blur. The crowd of spirits clapped and cheered. For a moment, Darren felt the best he had all day.

It was a merry sight. Spirits of all creeds, colours and kinds intermingled, talking and laughing. Nothing was missing. There was no hunger, no thirst, no hate. Love was there for all to see and share, but the will to go any further was a thing for the world they had left behind. There was no future to preserve, no desire to harm. The harm had already been done. This was a stopping place, on the way to somewhere else.

As the night wore on, the Morris men and women left. Sid and a few others lay on the grass and stared at the stars. Darren asked about the Morris dancers and how they'd got to be there. Sid told him.
"They were on a trip to a gig and their minibus turned over and burst into flames."
"Oh my God, that's horrendous!" Darren said.
"Yeah," said Sid, almost dismissively, then he continued,
"You'll be here long enough to hear all the stories about how people died. It will eventually wash over you because there's nothing you can do about it."

Darren had slept soundly on the grass against a hedge. He opened his eyes, stared at an electric-blue morning sky. He sat up slowly, watched the sun caress the trees, then, as their long shadows drove across the perfectly still countryside, he realised he was all alone. He didn't know why. It didn't matter. He soaked up the wonderful vista, like it was the only thing he had ever seen. The dew was heavy on the grass. It was cold but he was warm and dry. Inside his head, he thought it was all so crazy, but so damn beautiful. He started to cry. He wiped his eyes, then put his hand into his bag, pulled out his iPod, placed the earplugs in his ears and put it on shuffle. The Beatles' *Across the Universe* came on. He sat there, trying to find peace and realised he had all the ingredients he needed.

Darren wasn't sure what he really felt. It was like he'd arrived at a station somewhere for a connecting train but knew he had to wait for as long as it would take to catch the next one. He made his way back to the cornfield, to the Ley line where he had been the previous day with Sid. When he got there, he stared across to the other field. Although he knew he couldn't see the Ley line, he knew it was there, so he lifted up his hands and pushed them through, followed by the rest of his body. It felt like lots of little pins were stabbing him. Before he knew it, he was back by the side of the road, where all this started. This time it didn't take as long for his head and body to settle down.

As he sat there, he focused on some flowers that had been left, just by the edge of the road. This hit him hard. The sorrow was not like how he'd thought it might be. He felt for his mum and dad, yet he was somehow detached, almost as if someone had taken his need to grieve. He stared at the flowers and thought what a strange thing to do, kill flowers and leave them for the dead. *Cups,* by Lulu and the Lampshades played on his iPod. The chorus, "when I'm gone", kept going through his mind.

He needed to talk to someone, so he walked back to the bus stop and waited behind an old lady. He got on the bus. It never occurred to him that the bus would only stop if a living person wanted to get on or off. Darren stood holding a strap hanging from above. The bus was full. It was mostly kids going to school. A young girl in her school uniform was in the aisle, as she was getting off at the next stop. So were many others. Darren was in the way. He could barely move, so he tried to stand to one side. Each of the children piled off the bus, moving through Darren's body. He collapsed into a now empty seat and lay there, wrapping his arms around his chest. In the opposite seat, sat a young West Indian, looking across at Darren, who said,

"That'll do for the first time! You do get used to it! Next time breathe in and tighten the muscles. It's a bit like warm water rolling over you then, but if you're not ready for it, it hurts."

"Sid didn't tell me," croaked Darren. The man started laughing.

"You mean punk Sid?"

"Yes," Darren replied.

"He's an arse sometimes, but he knows an awful lot of what's going on."

Darren was recovering and sat up properly. The man slid across and shook his hand.

"My name's Ajay," he said adding "My friends call me Jay."

Darren nodded then studied Ajay. He was a good-looking, well-built man, who looked like he pumped iron. His Afro hair was tied, then bunched at the top with a band in red, green and yellow. Darren liked him immediately, then asked,

"How did you get to be here?"

The bus continued on its loop around the outskirts of Hereford. Jay explained,

"I'm an electrician. I was working at my sister's new salon. A bit of wiring needed some attention. I was there with my apprentice. I had let him do some of the work. I didn't know it at the time, but it was girl trouble. He'd fallen out with his girlfriend, was on his phone and wasn't concentrating. Trouble was, I was distracted by my sister. She said she would cut my hair, as you can see, not much cutting needed, so there I was, sat in conversation with her, as she cut my hair. She was so excited; the new shop was fully booked. I couldn't help but feel pleased for her. I had put the electricity back on. My apprentice was in the back, drinking coffee, texting.

Then I heard him shouting "Fire!" Smoke alarms went off.

I told my sister to get out of the shop, I ran into the back. The kitchen area was on fire. I grabbed a fire extinguisher and tried to put it out. My apprentice was near the door, so I said, "Call the fire brigade!" He slipped into the back yard which had a back entrance, and I did my best, but it needed professionals.

I ran out the front. My sister was being comforted by her assistant, so I went to my van parked across the road to get another fire extinguisher. It was then I thought I heard the fire engine. I turned, looked and saw a car coming towards me. It killed me

instantly."
Darren asked,
"What happened? Why did the car crash into you?"
Ajay continued,
"Two young lads had nicked a car; the police were in pursuit. As
the lads were coming down the street, they saw the flames and
smoke from the shop, which distracted them. They swerved
and smashed into the back of my van."

Darren sat open-mouthed and tried to take the story in.
"How did you know about the two young lads?"
"They told me."
Ajay then looked over his shoulder and pointed to the back of
the bus. Two young lads were sat there with their legs up on the
seats, chatting to each other. Ajay waved at them. So did Darren,
weakly, then he asked,
"How do feel about it?"
"Well, they're nice enough lads, both fourteen. They went to my
school. They told me they'd had a few spliffs, then had gone for a
ride in someone's car they'd nicked."
Darren asked,
"What did they say to you about the crash?"
Ajay replied,
"Not much. They just said sorry!"
A silence hung there, as the bus trundled along another B road
on its route around the countryside. Darren was beginning to
see the world according to ghosts. It put some of his thoughts
into perspective and it eased his mind even further. One thing
was for sure, he realised being dead left the emotions in limbo.
Darren, having taken his earplugs out to listen to Ajay, put them
back in and continued to listen to his iPod. He was thinking of
Vanessa and *Let Her Go* came on by Passenger.

Sanjita Singh was sitting two seats back down the bus, taking
notes. She had been a junior reporter for the local newspaper.
She was listening to Darren and Ajay. She already knew Ajay's

story, but she took notes anyway. At her side was a largish bag, with everything a reporter should have and more besides, as well as, of course, a mobile phone, which was of no use here. A couple of times she had wanted to take photos, but you can't take a picture of a ghost.

She had a plentiful supply of notebooks. Her boss was old-fashioned, he'd say 'Write it down on paper, then you know it comes from the heart.'
It wasn't until these last few months that she had understood what he had meant.
Sanjita had also noted her own death very accurately.
It happened on a really awful night in December. The city lights, along with the Christmas lights, gave a warm glow in an otherwise dim skyline. She had been helping out in her spare time at a hostel for the homeless. At first, it was just for a piece that she was compiling, maybe to publish. That's if her boss would let her. She was walking home after a long day, reporting then volunteering in a homeless shelter.
She lived with her mum and dad in a terraced house in the middle of the town. She could smell her mum's wonderful cooking, as she came in through the front door. Her supper would be waiting in a pot on top of the stove. She made herself some tea. Her mum came in from the living room and immediately chastised her for working too late.
"I suppose you've been working at the homeless shelter again."
She nodded, as she took a refreshing sip of her tea, then asked,
"Where are my brothers?"
"Both are upstairs, studying," her mum said.
"On their mobile phones more like."
"That may be," said mum, "But I know they will do their homework."
Sanjita's brothers were twins, both studying their A levels.
"Will you eat now?" her mum asked.
"Yes! Thanks mum!"
She sat down and ate the delicious, warming food. Her mum sat

with her, placed her hand on her daughter's and said,

"You can't save the world all by yourself, you know! There are superheroes who do that on the telly all the time."

Sanjita laughed. She always found her mum to be great company. When she had finished, her mum said,

"Don't work too late!"

She knew her daughter would probably be finishing another report to hand into the boss the next day.

Sanjita was working on an extensive report: a look into homelessness in the city. She had been working on it for months. She printed it out before she went to bed because her boss was old-fashioned. He wanted all his journalists' work on paper, not via the computer, so she piled the file into her bag, cleaned her teeth and collapsed into bed.

Next morning, bright and early, Sanjita got up; as always, before her brothers but never before her mum and dad. They were both at the kitchen table, drinking tea. Her dad had a convenience store, not far away, which they all used to live above but, as the years passed, money got easier, so they'd bought the house they were in now.

Sanjita sat down. There was peace for the moment. No-one spoke. One thing they had all learned was it's no good talking about personal stuff, when you were nearly ready to walk out of the door. So, the silence was welcome. That is, until her brothers came down. They charged into the kitchen, shirts and ties akimbo, threw their bags on to the floor, instantly asking their mum where stuff was. Their dad immediately said,

"Look for yourselves!"

Mum got up to help, and of course dad got annoyed. Sanjita sipped her tea. This was so normal, and she loved it. She stood up amid the mayhem, slipped into the hall, grabbed her bag, her warm coat and a scarf and said,

"I'm off."

She kissed her dad on the cheek. Her mum hugged her. She high fived her brothers, who laughed as they scooped cereal into their mouths.

Sanjita left the house. She was early. She wanted plenty of time to hand in her report to her editor. She had butterflies in her stomach. She walked down the road, which was relatively quiet, then onto a main road. It was a nice crisp morning, plenty of blue sky but really cold. She pulled up her scarf to her chin with her gloved hands and walked faster. She loved the sound of the city, the drone of the vehicles, here and there a robin singing, pin-pointing life and nature. The odd bushes and hedges, having hoarfrost, beautified the otherwise dark city surroundings.

She reached the underpass, where she had to go, because it was almost impossible to cross the main road. There was a slope that turned and then some steps, which she couldn't quite see until she turned. At the top sat a homeless man, with most of his worldly goods stretched out next to him.

Sanjita wasn't aware he was there and, as she turned to go down the steps, her foot caught on the cardboard layer stretched out underneath him. She tripped and went tumbling down to the bottom of the steps. There were twelve steps in all. She hit the last two with her head.

The homeless man woke, got up and saw what had happened. He moved down the stairs slowly, not being very awake and by far the worse for wear from too much alcohol the night before. He recognised her immediately and held her, blood pouring from the back of her head. He was apologising to her, as another person came by and called an ambulance.

Sanjita could remember the man with his long, dark hair and scraggy beard, and especially the warm tears that fell onto her face as he sobbed,

"Sorry, so sorry!"

Darren got up from the seat next to Ajay. He was going to talk to the boys at the back of the bus but stopped when he saw Sanjita writing. He sat in a seat opposite her with his legs in the aisle, then introduced himself. She told him her name and the fact she had been a reporter when she was alive, and how she had died. They talked and talked about their lives. Maybe in another life, their light might have been shared. Then, as the country bus was coming to a little village, they were all going to get off. Darren was puzzled.

"Why here?"

"This is where one of the Ley lines cuts across the county. We need to get off or we'll be sent back to where we died," explained Sanjita.

Darren got off the bus with the small group of spirits. The two young lads went off together, laughing and joking. Death seemed perfect for them. Sanjita, Darren and Ajay walked together. Darren rarely took out his earplugs. In the background, *Crazy Love,* by Van Morrison, was just finishing. The day was superb, the sun high and bright as they walked through the village. Sanjita was taking them somewhere. They walked past old timbered houses with their cottage gardens, foxgloves, forget-me-nots and rambling roses. It set the perfect picture; in the distance, a church with its spire piercing the luminous sky, was a sight to see.

"This is where two Ley lines cross," said Sanjita. "Holy and spiritual sites seem to adorn the British countryside."

They stood in the graveyard. Other spirits were there too, some sitting on walls, some even on gravestones. Flowers were dotted here and there, left by the loved ones of those long dead. Sanjita explained that some spirits just waited here or wherever they may have died and just patiently stayed for the fading. Some would move on quickly, usually those that had no family to speak of, so no-one to keep them earthbound.

They walked up the path to the church, reaching the great wooden door which was opened by a living couple who were coming out of the church, allowing Sanjita and the other two to slip inside, joining more people and spirits. The Ley line cut through the middle of the church, so some spirits were on one side of the church and some on the other side, almost like a wedding where different families sit in different pews.

Of course, here and there, living people were quietly walking around, talking to each other. Darren took out his ear plugs. He thought it was divine. The sun shone through the illuminated windows on a religious scene, giving light and catching dust that had been disturbed by the living and the dead.

Although the other spirits could be seen from their side of the church, nothing could be heard. You could see the odd spirit trying to communicate but to no avail. The Ley line was definitely as good as a castle wall.

Sanjita sat towards the back of the church, as did Darren, but Ajay walked around, looking at the tombs. Darren started talking to Sanjita. He felt comfortable with her as it seemed that she was with him, almost as if they had found an inner peace to share.

He asked her about the homeless she worked with and the things she had written. She told him that she had been back, but only briefly. They had named the drop-in centre after her and the article she had written got published in full, giving an insight into how bad things were. The city tackled the problem of homelessness and reduced it in six months.

Darren was impressed.

"How do *you* feel about it, Sanjita?"

"Like everything here, it's dulled. We can feel, we care, but we have no effect. We're between here and the next place, so we are just waiting, watching, remembering.

They sat side by side, silently watching the sun slowly move the spirits around them into the sunny afternoon. It seemed the perfect moment for Darren to replace one of his ear plugs. He turned to Sanjita.

"Listen to this."

Sanjita took the other earplug and placed it in her ear. *Over the Rainbow,* by Israel Kamakawiwo'ole was playing.

Eventually, Darren spoke.

"Were there many flowers after you died?"

There was a pause, then Sanjita said,
"Yes loads, all down by the underpass and on the roadside."
"There was just one yesterday where I died," said Darren, to which Sanjita replied,
"I guess not many know you have died yet, Darren."
He smiled at her and said,
"I need to see."
Even though he knew that walking into the Ley line would make him feel awful, it was the quickest way to get back.
"Bye for now," she said. He was gone.

He sat at the side of the road, his brain scrambled, his body shivering. Moby's *We Are All Made of Stars* was playing. This time, he was over it quickly. As he came round, he rubbed his eyes and saw more than a dozen bunches of flowers, just for him. He felt better, though the feeling wasn't of great loss or pain; he just needed to see that people missed him. Something curious was going on inside him. It seemed that within a couple of days, he had found all the spirits there were strangely incomplete, but still very much functioning in this other world. He contemplated the fact that the world he had been very much a part of before, had no knowledge or concept of how death works. He spent that evening reading the cards that were with the flowers. He couldn't see one from Vanessa.

Darren stayed there for days by the side of the road, happy to be on his own. More flowers appeared, left by people he hardly knew. Then, one misty morning, he got up and made his way to the bus stop. On the bus he found Sid, languishing across a couple of seats, a cigarette in his mouth. Darren sat down. There were quite a few old-age pensioners travelling on the bus at the time. When he saw Darren, Sid said,
"There are a few candidates on the bus today. Do you bet at all? Pick one! I'll give you a fag if you get it right!"
He then started laughing. Darren said nothing for a moment, then asked,

"Where's the crematorium? Is it inside the Ley lines?"
Sid got down, looked at Darren and said,
"Yeah."
"Where is it?" Darren asked.
"You catch the bus on the other side of the road going the other way. It'll take you there."
"Thanks," said Darren.
As Darren got off at the next stop, Sid wished him "Good luck," whilst *Mrs. Robinson* was playing on his iPod.

Darren stood on the other side of the road, after dodging the cars. Whilst watching the cars speeding by, as he waited for the bus, his mind was still in a muddle. He contemplated the people driving, thinking, *do they realise how close they are to being me?*

When the bus turned up, several people got off. Darren stood back then jumped on. He went to the back seats where two old people were sat and said, "Hello."
They were holding hands. Both had dressing-gowns and slippers on. They looked at Darren, beaming with large wrinkly smiles and, as with most elderly people, they began chatting straight away.
"I'm Rose, this is James," the old lady said. "Do you remember Rosie and Jim on the tv?"
Darren shook his head, then Rose said,
"Oh well, that's what all our friends used to call us."
There was a brief silence.
"How did you end up here together?" asked Darren.
"We made a suicide pact," explained Rosie. "James was getting forgetful, and I was in bed all the time from various illnesses."
James then interrupted,
"It was the only way! We knew we wouldn't want to be left alone so, one night, we took all the pills we had, then drank a few sherries. That's all we remember."
Rosie gave a beaming, attractive smile, then she stood up and said,

"Look! I can stand!"

She did a little jig, then Jim recited a times table, before saying, "It's the best we have felt in years!"

"How would your children have felt about you committing suicide?" asked Darren.

James replied,

"We had no children! Most our relatives have died or moved abroad."

As the bus travelled on, Darren saw a sign out of the corner of his eye. It said Crematorium, so he shook both their hands and stood up to go. Rosie held his hand a few moments longer and said,

"You seem sad. I can see it in your eyes."

He looked at her then said,

"It's a long story."

"Ok," she said. "Next time!"

Darren smiled at her, then she said,

"We're off to the shops! I do like to walk now!"

Darren left the bus and made the long walk up the drive to the crematorium. As he walked, he saw beautiful cherry trees having just lost their flowers, as well as Rhododendron trees in full bloom, vast lawns, edged by green forest and, here and there, herbaceous borders. A large water feature with palms sat before the large, modern crematorium building, softening its architectural features. *What a place to come to,* thought Darren, as he got closer to the main building.

As he walked into the red brick and glass building, a ceremony was taking place. He sat at the back and watched. It was all very emotional, but Darren wasn't moved. Here and there, scattered amongst the living, he could see other spirits. He acknowledged them with a nod of the head or a slight smile. He sat there all day, watching each party come in to sit, to watch and listen, then cremate the mortal remains of their loved ones.

When the day had ended, the staff busied themselves for the next day. There was almost too much fun, as they chatted about this and that, the cleaners, the admin staff... It seemed like all that sadness had to go somewhere. Darren felt quite uplifted by it all, as he listened.

Darren left them to it. The odd spirit, just like him, started to walk the gardens. He didn't want to communicate so he kept to himself. Next morning, after spending the night under a giant oak, Darren found himself sitting at the back in the cremator- ium again, waiting, watching. Then he saw Sanjita. She came and sat by his side, asking,
"How long have you been here?"
"Since yesterday."
"You're on at three pm," Sanjita whispered, even though no-one could hear her.
"How do you know?"
She looked at him and said,
"I am a journalist!"
He smiled, she smiled back. He felt relieved, as he had not been certain that his parents would have chosen to have him cre- mated.

The time went by. Sanjita and Darren watched, as each cere- mony came and went. Darren had turned off his iPod so he could hear everything that was going on, as well as all the music that was being played. That seemed to be almost an anthem to people's lives. So many, so varied.
Always look on the bright side of life, by Eric Idle, stuck in his head. He wouldn't have it for himself but the thought of it was funny and, somehow, appropriate.
Close to three o'clock, Sanjita asked Darren to go outside. They stood as the hearse turned up. He looked at Sanjita and said,
"Did you come here after you died, to see the ceremony?"
She looked at him.
"Yes, everyone does," she said, "it seems almost like a rite of passage."

As the undertakers were opening the hearse to get the casket out, Darren saw Sid, Ajay, the young lads off the bus and even Rosie and James, walking towards him, as well as, amazingly, the Morris Dancers in full blacked-out faces and colourful ribboned jackets.

Darren and the others gathered round. The Morris Dancers took up positions. As an accordion and a violin played, they danced for him. Darren was moved. He cried for himself.

They followed the bearers into the building and sat, this time closer to the front, as did all their spirit friends. Outside, he could still hear the Morris Dancers. It was magical.

His dad spoke first. Darren could see the pain in his Dad's eyes, as his words gave reason to Darren's life. The words were beautiful and obviously heartfelt. He was followed by Vanessa who added her own words about their burgeoning love. Darren watched Vanessa as she spoke, but it was like everyone else was a million miles away, so untouchable. Their wonderful words somehow joined them but also severed the connection. One song that they played during the ceremony was *Yellow* by Coldplay. Darren knew his mum and dad loved the song, as he did too. By the end of the ceremony, he knew that this part was as important as anything: to live with death.

Tears flowed. Darren's too. And even Sanjita's.

Afterwards, when everyone had gone, Darren went outside with the others. They started to walk around the gardens, taking in the flowers that lay in tribute to Darren. Sid, Ajay, the two lads and old Rosie and James all sat on the grass, singing along to the Morris Dancers' songs. Other spirits also sat and joined in.

Darren and Sanjita walked off, talking quietly to each other, down an avenue of flowering late spring trees. As he walked, Darren was humming one of the songs his mum and dad had picked: *I'll Find My Way Home,* by Jon and Vangelis.

In life, there is always going to be death, so it seems important to find your song and sing it.

POPS

The sky was the perfect turquoise blue of early summer. Up high, circling the heavens, were two beautiful birds of prey. They were harnessing the warm air thermals to keep the movement of their wings to a minimum, being ever alert to any creatures that may attempt to move on the ground. A plaintiff cry could be heard from them, which seemed to dominate the countryside they oversaw. Down there, there was a small cottage with a couple of acres of garden. Attached to it, looking like a jetty pushing out into a green sea, was an old station platform, unused for many years. The end of the line for the train station became the end of the line for the beautiful village that surrounded it many years ago.

Dotted around the station, there were small houses that had fallen into disrepair, overgrown with tall weeds, bushes and trees. Further on, there was a big house with many outbuildings, the only other thing that looked lived in.

The birds of prey which flew lower over the disused rail track were looking for a kill. One of them had spied something moving in the cottage gardens.

Something troubled Amos; a darkness he tried never to think of. It was in the form of an echo in his head. His daily conversation with his wife's photograph brought it to the front of his mind. As he sat resting for a moment, his thoughts wandered. A shadow cut across the ground not far off into his beautiful cottage garden; a bird of prey, who he knew to be a red kite, one of a pair that often circled high up above his house. As he landed on the ground, the bird stared at Amos who watched him carefully. He never tired of seeing them, especially when it was up close like this. The bird lowered its head as if to make sure whatever he had caught was secure, then, with such pure majesty, took to the air and flew away.

This interruption in Amos's thought process was brief, but it imprinted itself into his head. He was alone again, sat in his garden, looking upward to the sky. The red kites were back up there, after their small breakfast. He shielded his old eyes from the sun's glare as they flew higher.

Amos was showing his age; life had caught up with him, being in his early seventies. He was still able to move around, but his arthritis was taking its toll. The old wooden chair that he was sitting on was by far the worse for wear, after being left out in all the elements. Like him, it was showing its great age. The loose shirt and old baggy trousers he was wearing kept him cool. He waved his old hat backwards and forwards to fend off the irritating flies. They too were feeling hot.

Butterflies whisked past him, as did bumble bees on their way to nectar heaven, the hollyhocks and lavender, the banquet of the day. Like the bees, Amos mumbled to himself, words of wonderment of what he saw, although he'd seen it time and time again. He reached into his misty mind to retrieve the memories that haunted him. These memories that he treasured were not all bad ones, but at the moment they were tinged with a fog that he was finding hard to see through. The abundance of nature around him, eased him back: the subtlety, the beauty, its endless wonder.

Again, it came to him suddenly, like an echo from sometime in the past, then it was as clear as the red kite who had not long flown away.

A figure of a young girl stood before Amos's Japanese maple. The tree was around eight foot tall, planted by Amos and Victoria almost forty years ago. The colours were wondrous to behold, it contributed such beauty to the garden. Sitting in the branches there was a robin, who seemed to be singing to the girl. The girl was about five years old. She looked towards Amos and smiled. She was beautiful with shoulder-length blond hair, bright cheeks and dressed in a flowery yellow dress. She started to dance, lightly moving from toe to toe. Words came from her mouth; he couldn't hear them, but he knew what she was saying inside his head, as if there was an echo resounding in his mind.

"Look at me, Pops! Look at me! I'm a flower dancing!"

Then he heard his own voice calmly saying,

"Yes, yes, I can see you."

Inside, he had a warm feeling. Even the robin seemed moved and sang louder in the tree, then the apparition was gone.

Amos stood, carefully redistributing his weight to the joints he was more sure of, with the help of his walking stick, his trusty companion. Once upright, he was more assured. His old cottage at his back, he surveyed his life's work. His cottage garden that he still managed to maintain with some difficulty, he slowly walked through. Yes, there were weeds, here and there, but that was always the case, he was no slave to the extinction of such things. After all, they had a place. He just tried to think that beauty came in all forms. Perhaps, he thought, one day the dandelion would be like the Mona Lisa, idolised for its far-off beauty.

He adjusted his sun hat. Like him, it was old. Most of its frayed stitches were lost through ancient sweat and constant use, which made it look somewhat askew on his almost hairless head. The hair that he had was as white as snow.

Amos had a cheerful disposition. The lines around his mouth were more of a smile than that of sadness, unless he looked as far back as when his wife died of a heart attack nearly thirty years ago. A photograph of her hung in his living room. Every day, he kissed it, sharing his love and affection. These moments filled his mind with happiness.

He walked on down a red brick path, at his sides, the colours of the flowers like rainbows on his shoulders. He heard crows in the distance, a reminder of autumn and winter. Somehow, in the summer, their cries, like their colour, edged the day with black. Perhaps this was unfair, but it was one early dark December morning when his wife was taken. His thoughts always strayed as he heard the crows. On that fateful morning he'd heard their cries as he sat on a wooden chair in the garden, after she had passed away. The crows were like a black heavenly choir, chorusing her going.

He wished them no harm and, in some ways, saw them as a way of mourning her loss.

Amos's vegetable garden sat against a tall wall, where vegetables of all varieties were sheltered from the weather, especially the wind. The garden was wrapped around the cottage, the best part of which faced south. On a good day, it was usually bathed in sunshine.

Amos loved the spring, summer and autumn. At one time the winter was his friend, a time to recoup, regenerate, but now it was a darkness in his heart. Nevertheless, he had found comfort in it, in his home and in his garden.

It being early summer, birdsong filled the air. A friend had come to see him. A robin sat upon a piece of wall that was in need of repair, singing its heart out. Amos sometimes thought the robin was singing just for him. He would always stop, listen and watch the little bird. The robin normally was impeccably dressed in his red waistcoat, but at the moment he looked slightly the worse for wear, having recently raised a brood of chicks with his partner. Even so, you could never take it away from the robin:

he had a magnificent voice.

Again, the apparition of the young girl danced down the dry, dusty path. The robin took to the air as if to mimic the glorious moment. Amos watched patiently, then smiled at the sheer joy of it.
"Follow me, Pops! Dance with me!"
Again, he saw her lips move, but could not hear her voice. Somehow, he knew what she was saying. His heart fluttered at her happiness. He and the robin seemed to dance along in unison. After all, how could you not do what a pretty little girl would ask you to do? In his frailness, he shimmied from side to side. She smiled as she danced, then, as quickly as she came, she was gone.

An old fork sat against the warming wall as the sun beat down on it. Amos grasped it and carefully plunged it into the dry earth. Not far down, it was damp enough; after a few turns, a few tasty worms could be found. He gathered them up. Without a second thought, the robin landed on his hand, eating the worms in quick succession. The robin retreated to the wall, almost as if to say "More please." Amos obliged. This was a regular thing between Amos and the robin, for more than ten minutes or until the robin was full. Then as if to say thank you, he would sing his happy tune. Satisfied, he then flew off.

Amos surveyed his garden. All things were as they should be: green beans were halfway up their polls, the fine feathery stalks of the carrots waving slowly in the warm breeze, onions in a straight line, albeit in an untidy way. He smiled inwardly at his attention to uniformity. His father would have been proud.
He unlatched the wooden gate that lead out into a beautiful orchard. The blossoms on the trees had only just turned and fallen, the ground below was now covered in a pink and white carpet. His mind drifted. It seemed captured by the little girl that appeared and created the strange echo in his head. He knew it to be a memory: it somehow had more resonance than his everyday

conversations with his wife's photograph.

Slowly he walked between the apple and pear trees, breathing in the sweet smell that was still lingering. Along the far edge of the field, he meandered, then slipped through a gap in the hedge. He looked down the path that went on for some distance in one direction. It was overgrown with bushes and brambles. Even so, it could clearly be seen as a disused rail track.

Amos stopped at the old buffers at the end of the station, now, no more than rotten wood and rusting metal, overrun with weeds, the station long gone. A train, at one time, would have sat there waiting for its passengers, gently chuffing to itself, eagerly waiting to take them wherever they wished to go. He walked up the abandoned track, hearing the noises of a ghostly train, almost being able to see his father framed in the steam from a train as it pulled away. He stretched his head back steadying himself with his stick. He heard the red kites up above him screeching, their shadows rushing over the trees above his head.

The stationmaster's cottage was where he had lived all his life, with his mother, father, brothers and sisters. His father was the stationmaster until Dr Beeching closed the branch line, like many others, in 1963.

Amos, the youngest child, was a teenager when his father gave him the job as a porter. Twelve months later, the line was closed. The lifeline that the railway had been, was unceremoniously taken away from the village that wrapped around the railway track. All that was left was the stationmaster's cottage. The houses in the village slipped into disrepair over the years. The children who had lived there grew up, left to find work elsewhere, then their parents grew old and would eventually die. Most of the houses belonged to the big house and farm, the owner of which had no children, so, when he and his wife passed away, there was no-one left to maintain the properties. Over time the village houses became shells, overrun with weeds. In some cases, even trees grew where once there had been pretty cottages and gardens.

There were no takers to come and rejuvenate them, because the trains had gone, the track had been dismantled. It was dead, it was literally the end of the line for nearly everything.

Amos's father was given severance pay when the track was closed, so he bought the house. Unfortunately, Amos's brothers and sisters had to leave home to find work, to find another life elsewhere, the big city being the most popular place to go. Amos, being the youngest, had stayed at home with his mother, while his father had gone off to find work. As Amos grew older, he did small jobs in the area where he could, until his mother became infirm and needed constant attention. This was difficult for him, especially when his father died suddenly. His mother needed help, so her doctor organised a nurse to come and look after her. It was love at first sight. As she walked in the front door, something just clicked between Amos and Victoria, the nurse.

Not long after, someone bought the big house and the farm. That was when Amos got work helping to rebuild it.

He and Victoria married in a small church not many miles from their home. A few members of his and her family attended, neither of them having had many friends. Their world was a small place, never really needing other people's company, so they settled to their rural pasture with an ease that suited them both.

"Chloe, who you talking to?" Chloe danced around and around in circles, her yellow dress swirling in the warm breeze. With the backdrop of tall weeds, dandelions, and tangled hollyhocks, it was a picture to behold. She slowed down to stop and continued to talk out loud.

"I think Chloe has an imaginary friend," said Tyler, her dad, to Nova, her mum. They were still sorting through the boxes after the move. The cottage they had bought at auction, needed a lot of work inside and out, but it was in the most beautiful spot in the country. Tyler had a few weeks off from work, so they could all settle in.

It was a beautiful day. Tyler was watching Chloe, while nursing a cup of coffee. They had moved to the country for peace and quiet, grasping the chance to get away from the rat race. Tyler and Nova had a passionate need to live in green space and maybe survive off the land. At the moment though, Tyler was in between two places. Being in computers, he was developing ways of using them in his desire to help create a more resourceful life. Of course, the computer couldn't do this on its own. He was hoping to develop programmes to initiate it. Tyler wasn't a fool; he knew it would all be hard work, mental as well as physical, but he and Nova were keen to have a go.

The cottage they had bought was a mess. It was reflected in the price they paid for it. Even so, they were keen to turn the old station-master's cottage into a wonderful place to live. Meanwhile Tyler had to work for someone else, using his car to take him backwards and forwards to the city where he worked. Nova had given up her job to become a full-time mother, not that there was any work where they had moved to.

The community, if you could call it that, was a few new houses on an even newer road in the middle of nowhere. All that said, they were all happy to be there. Nova was going to home school Chloe, something in many ways she was looking forward to. As far as Chloe was concerned, she was as happy as any five-year-old child would be in the garden of Eden.

Amos slowly walked up onto the station platform, which was still in good order. He had seen to it that it was swept clean every day, although the wooden ticket office and waiting room was long gone, having been used for firewood over the years. Of course, there were weeds in the cracks of the old flagstones, dandelions had flourished in the space they'd acquired. In some ways, the platform looked so much better for it. The old station cottage backed onto the platform, nestled like a harbour against a sea of nature. As he climbed on the platform, he remembered the good times: a steam train would come in, in a few moments many people would be climbing on and off. To him, it seemed busy, but the truth was it was a quiet backwater that a few families and farmers needed to keep in touch with the world outside. Even though he was a teenager at the time, the memories flowed back. He still had his whistle and the flag that his dad had given to him when he first started the job.

He picked up a broom that lay against a rusting metal fence. Very slowly, he swept the platform.

The apparition that was the young girl danced along, her dress seeming to give her flight. The warm air made it appear as if she was a mirage on a stage that was the platform. Slowly, she stopped and turned to Amos.

"Why are you doing that, Pops?"

The question made him pause and stand for a moment, the sun overhead making his shadow almost unnoticeable. He retrieved a handkerchief from his old baggy trousers, then removed the old hat on his head and wiped away the sweat. He couldn't seem to answer. The question was like someone had stopped the clocks.

"Are you ok, Pops?"

He stood there like a statue, one that looked as if it needed to sit down. He mumbled to himself something that couldn't be defined.

"Pardon?" she asked.

Amos needed to rest, so he placed the broom against the fence, then walked slowly towards the front of the station house. It took a few minutes, the path being difficult through overgrown bushes.

The wild birds around the cottage were quieter now, because it was getting hotter, and they were tired after feeding their bigger families.

Amos opened the front door of the old station cottage. Even though it was a cottage, it had a Victorian feel to it. He walked in and it was immediately cooler inside, the dark hallway a welcome break from the hot sun. The place had seen so many people over the years walk through the front doors. Now it was just him, plus the odd ghostly memory. He sat in an old chair in the front room that his mother had called the best room, a place they hardly ever used when he was younger. Even though he was now old, he still loved the feeling of defiance, because he used the room all the time.

He reminisced as he cooled, breathing less heavily now, wondering how his brothers and sisters were, all scattered to far-off places in the world. He didn't envy them. After all, there was nowhere better than this, as far as he was concerned. He looked up at the wall beside the old open fireplace. Photographs that hung there were of his mother, father, brothers and sisters, proving somehow that they had all existed. The ones of Victoria and himself were lower down. His heart rose to the memory of them, only to fall as he looked lower. This one was of a little girl, five years old, with shoulder length hair, a beautiful smile and wearing a lovely flowery dress. A tear came to his eye.

Chloe was having fun in the overgrown garden. The paths, though weedy, were easy enough to walk along. Chloe sang to herself, enjoying the beautiful sunny day.

Tyler and Nova, after a busy morning, decided to look at the garden. After all, it was the most important part about buying the property. They knew that Chloe was safe enough, because the garden was closed in, the hedges being really overgrown. They called Chloe. There was no answer. This didn't trouble them. After all, the garden was very large. Making their way around, they saw Chloe dancing by a long wall, attached to which was an old rickety gate. She was talking to herself. The strange thing was, there was a robin that seemed to be listening to her on the nearby wall which needed repair. The robin seemed to interact with her, as she danced around and around.

Her parents stood still, watching the animated conversation she was having. The dancing that followed was so joyous, then she stopped and danced towards them. She seemed to be so happy, laughing, singing and enjoying the garden. They were happy too, but both of them felt a little concerned in some strange way.

Amos was sat head in hands, nursing his memories, when he heard the echo in the kitchen.

"Pops! Where are you? Look!"

Amos stood, feeling better for the rest, finding it easier to stand with his walking stick, then he made his way into the kitchen. It was brightly lit. The sun, having moved around the house, now shone through the kitchen windows. The girl was sitting at the kitchen table.

"Look, the teddy bear's ripped!"

Amos sat, his frail figure cooling, beads of sweat still upon his old, wrinkled head. His fingers worked their way along the seams of the scruffy teddy bear after she gave it to him. She sang to herself gently, as she sat opposite him.

"What is the song you're singing?" he asked.

"You know what it is! *Rose* sings it all the time!"

For a moment, Amos's head spun. He found it difficult to understand what was happening, but still he got up and moved towards a drawer, retrieved a needle and some cotton, his arthritic bony fingers still nimble enough to stitch. He passed the well-worn teddy back to her.

"Thanks so much Pops, it's back to being happy again."

Amos got up to make himself some tea, then opened the back door to look out into the glorious garden, especially at the magnificent maple tree. The sights and sounds of the day swallowed up his thoughts as the apparition ebbed away.

Chloe was in her bed when her mum and dad came in to tell her a story. They gently asked her about who she was talking to in the garden earlier.

"Were you talking to the robin today, Chloe?"

She looked at them quizzically.

"No, I was talking to Pops. Pops was talking to the robin."

She said it in a matter a fact way, sighing as if she was impatient with the question.

"Who's Pops?" her mum asked. More sighs could be heard from Chloe.

"He's the man who lives here. He's a bit like grandad, but he's older I think."

She looked a little confused, then said as an afterthought,

"Yes, he is, his hair is so white, like snow."

Tyler and Nova were struck dumb for the moment. They shared a look with each other, not knowing whether to pursue with more questions.

"I want to go to sleep now, I'm tired!"

"You must be, sweetheart! You haven't stopped all day."

As they left her to go to sleep, they both put it down to the new surroundings and long hot sunny day.

The sun dipped lower in the sky. Amos moved from the kitchen outside into the shade of the large maple tree. The red to orange colours twinkled as the sun shone through the leaves. He looked up into it, feeling as if it was calling him.

The apparition stood beside him, looking up into the multi-layered colourful canopy.

"It's like an umbrella, Pops!"

"Yes, it is, like a sun umbrella," he answered.

She held the little teddy bear in her hands.

"What is its name?" she asked.

"Tatty, it belonged to my daughter, *Rose*." His voice tailed off, as if he'd suddenly seen a ghost.

As he looked at the apparition that now stood before him, he realised that something was not quite right. A far-off look came over his face, then robin broke the spell and started singing.

"Why do you look so sad, Pops?"

The robin sat among the branches of the beautiful tree and sang even louder like robins often do. They both then listened to his wonderful voice.

Chloe was up early singing in her bed. Her mum and dad came in fascinated by the sound of her voice. They saw her sat up, playing with a little teddy, one they didn't recognise.

"Where did you find the teddy, Chloe?" asked Nova.

"Can I look at it, sweetie?" Chloe gave it to her.

"Pops fixed it in the kitchen yesterday. He said its name is Tatty."

Nova ran her finger along the seams where there had been a repair.

"So, Pops was in the kitchen with you yesterday. Where were me and

your dad?"
"You were upstairs, putting my bed together."
They looked at each other, then realised that Chloe had spent a lot of time on her own, the day before.
Tyler was thinking "Where are we going with this?" Nova looked at him. They shared the same feeling. Chloe was never like this normally. Pops, the house, the garden seemed to have wrapped her up in some sort of fantasy.
"After he'd swept the station platform," continued Chloe," he was hot and tired, so he had a little rest. I asked him to fix Tatty, then he made some tea,"
Tyler and Nova's mouths dropped open, it was if there was another world going on around them, a world they couldn't hear or see. They were spiritual people, but they were taken aback by the current events. So much so, that Tyler decided to contact their solicitors, when they were open, to see if he could find out more about the history of the cottage.

The nights were long and arduous for Amos. It was never a good time for him. Memories, good and bad, permeated his thoughts. Since his wife died, he rarely ever slept upstairs. He had a bed of sorts in the front room, downstairs, among all his photographs. During this time, his mind slipped back to when he and Victoria had planted the maple tree in the garden. Ever since she'd passed away, every morning he was there outside looking at it, rain or shine. He would stare at its amazing form and beauty; the memory would then trickle back. The trouble was his mind was slipping more and more. Some days he found it difficult to remember why the tree was there at all.

Nova watched Chloe, as she played outside, a white sun hat on her head, lotion on her skin. The day was as wonderful as the day before, a slight breeze cooling the air. Nova sang, as she tidied the kitchen. It had an old-world charm to it which she loved, like the rest of the cottage. Until they were absolutely certain what they wanted to do with it, they were both happy to leave it as it was.

Amos sat again under the maple tree, feeding the robin bits of broken biscuits. He whistled to the robin every time he darted off to the tree. He then would come back for more biscuits. Amos was sat on his old wooden garden chair, his legs apart, leaning down, constantly talking to the little bird. The chores of gardening were put to one side, as he enjoyed a drink of tea and biscuits with his best friend. These things he had done for many years. Sometimes he wondered how long robins lived, but he wasn't certain how many years the robin had been his friend. He tried not to think about it. All he wanted to do was enjoy the day, almost like it would be his last.

Chloe twirled around, her dress was like that of a spinning top. She laughed, then she stopped, the giddiness made her wobble from side to side, which she loved.

"Careful," said Amos, "you'll fall over and hurt yourself."
These words were like the echo inside his head, as the apparition danced before him.
She did it again, shouting,
"Look, Pops, faster! Faster! Faster!"

Chloe spun even faster, then, as if in slow motion, fell towards the brick path. Nova saw her from the kitchen window as she fell and ran as fast as she could into the garden to try and catch her, but Chloe seemed to have been caught by some invisible force. Nova stopped yards from her daughter, then waited, captivated, as Chloe hung gently in the air. Slowly, she was placed back on the ground. Chloe was standing again, alone, apart from the robin who seemed to circle around her head.
Chloe was talking to someone, but there was no-one there. Nova tried to communicate with Chloe who seemed entranced, locked in a conversation.

Amos was on his knees, crying after catching Chloe. He held Chloe tightly, the distant echo was with him, the memory sharp and painful.

"Pops, it's ok, Rose is happy. So happy that you have remembered."

Amos released Chloe.

"Yes, I do remember Rose, my daughter."

The peaceful garden stood almost like it was captive to the distant memory and indeed it was.

Amos kissed Chloe on the cheek. Now he knew what the echo was inside his head: what he saw before him was not his daughter. Although the pain was deep, he knew it was time to go.

He smiled at Chloe, stood with the aid of his walking stick and moved off down the path, his tread slow and premeditated. He smelled his many roses on the way, pausing to take in everything for the last time.

Tyler joined Nova in the garden with news from the solicitor. Nova was now holding Chloe, who was waving to something or someone as Nova held her tight. They all stood there as the day seemed to go fast forward. Magically, it was twilight.

"Come with me! Come with me!" Chloe pulled on her parents' hands. "Come on!" she insisted.

She impatiently steered them down the garden path. They followed, fascinated by the events that were unfurling. Amos and the robin were up ahead. Chloe could see them; all that her parents could see was the robin weaving back and forth. Amos stopped at the old rickety garden gate, the sun now creating long shadows. A fine mist moved among the trees and thickened in the old orchard. Amos turned, as he opened the gate, then a young girl looking so similar to Chloe took Amos's hand. Amos was happy, a big smile spread across his face. He waved to Chloe and blew her a kiss. Chloe waved back, she was happy, too. As if to celebrate, she danced and twirled around, stopping only to wave and say,

"Goodbye, Pops, goodbye Rose."

Tyler and Nova were mesmerised and hypnotised by Chloe as she acted so strangely. Her actions and that of the robin seemed to be affected by someone or something that they couldn't see. The only thing they could make out was the swirling mist inside the orchard.

Suddenly, as quickly as the mist descended, it was gone.

Chloe looked up at her mum and dad.
"Will you teach me how to whistle, Dad?"
Tyler wasn't expecting the question, after what had just taken place. Without hesitation, he answered.
"Yes, of course I will, but why do you want to learn?"
"Because Pops said if you learn to whistle, it won't be long before you have a robin to feed worms to. Maybe then you can even make it your friend."
"Of course I will, sweetheart. Pops was very wise,"
Both her parents were still overcome by everything that had just happened. Obviously, there were questions, but who could possibly answer them?
"How did you know that the old man was called Pops?" her dad asked.
Chloe looked at him puzzled as if it was the strangest question ever.
"Because Rose told me, silly!"
As Chloe danced off, she sang to herself, her shadow now her only companion, apart from Tatty who was held tightly in her hand.

Tyler told Nova of Amos Brownlow, who'd owned the house originally with his wife Victoria, the story of how they'd lost their five-year-old daughter, when she fell and cracked her head on the brick path. Amos had always blamed himself for her death, because his mind was occupied at the time, while he was busy attending to his garden. He'd managed to keep her alive for a while, but by the time the doctor had arrived, she'd passed away.
"The maple tree was planted in her memory," he added.

As they walked back to the house, Tyler and Nova felt a perfect calm, something inside that was impossible to explain, almost certainly impossible to believe. It made them both feel like they were in heaven. Chloe continued to dance and sing in the dimming light, the turquoise sky having given way to the moon and stars.
At the kitchen door, they all looked up at the heavens, the stars being the perfect backdrop to the magic that had taken place.
"I think it's time for bed for all of us, Chloe," said her mum.

*"Could you tell me and Tatty a story about Pops and Rose?" asked
Chloe.*
Her mum and dad looked at each other and smiled.
"Yes, of course, sweetheart," they chorused, almost in harmony.

*As they slipped into the house, the robin started to sing joyously in
the maple tree.*

In that moment, when the earth gives itself up to the darkness
that night brings, the ground cools, flowers sleep and human-
ity rests, if it can. What of the spirit that is to wake no more,
because existence has been stolen from it? Is it possible that it
waits and lives a life that's not life at all? Maybe it becomes an
echo that needs to be heard and perhaps that echo is searching
for someone to help it on its way to some other place.

THE REINCARNATION OF JOE

Joe felt old and he was old. He was 68. He had heard all the cheerful words.

"You're not old, not these days. You'll get to 80 or even 90." Trouble was, when Joe woke, (that's if he ever slept, which in itself was a problem), then he would feel like a man who was far older. He was not a tall man, about 5 foot 7 inches, stocky and strong. He had a charm about him; with a cheeky glint in his eye and a warm involving smile, he was easy to talk to, a sort of man's man. He would often be found in the pub with a few friends and, if there weren't any around, he would somehow find someone to engage with, to talk with and laugh about life.

Joe had had a very physical life; his work was sometimes back-breaking. As a builder, he'd done most of the trades - bricklaying, carpentry, plastering, plumbing - he had turned his hand to nearly everything. So now, his body was aching most of the time. Yes, he'd retired, but to survive in this dislikable society, he couldn't just stop. He had to work, at least a few days a week, to help pay bills.

Joe worked part-time for his son, who had taken up the baton in the shadow of his father and was, to be fair, doing a fine job and better than him. This made Joe content for two reasons, one, his son was ably employed and two, the said son had taken all the pressure off Joe's shoulders. Despite only working three days a week, Joe had found, with the onset of a few medical problems - arthritis, an under-active thyroid, other aches and pains - that he needed to cut down his working days to two.

Joe was married to Anna, who he would call Annabelle when he was angry, and, to equal it up, she would call him Joseph in return. These arguments broke out infrequently, but when they did, they were both tested as to who would weaken first. Usually it was Joe, who couldn't cope with the animosity.
The making-up was always the best bit.
Their world was at peace; their son, Gabriel, was happy as a builder, whilst their younger child, Ava, was a teacher in a primary school. Gabriel and Ava were both married. There was talk of grandchildren, but up to now that was it. Neither Joe nor Anna wished to push them to have kids, clearly wanting Gabriel and Ava to enjoy life first, just like they had done.

Joe would often wake from an imperfect sleep, frequently experiencing exhausting dreams that led to him kicking or punching wildly. He blamed his age and his medication.
He was on small blue tablets with a long name that he couldn't pronounce, which were supposed to relax his muscles, but he wasn't sure they did, so, sometimes, he would take Ibuprofen or paracetamol as well, for his insufferable neck pain. This seemed to heighten the bad dreams.

One night, Joe had the most vivid dream, as he often did. This one, like all the others, he shared with his wife, the next day.
She was used to it and always listened.

Then, one morning, he said to Anna, as he awoke from a bad dream,
"I suppose that dreams are a release of anxiety, a way for the

body to come to terms with life's highs and lows."

As usual, Anna listened, but said nothing.

Later that day, Joe found himself washing his hands in the bathroom. He stared at himself, studying his face in the mirror and remembered when he was a young man, how smooth his skin was, apart from the odd pimple. Now it looked like a bike track. For some reason, he didn't know why, he didn't feel or look like himself and that was disconcerting.

As he studied the age around his eyes, he questioned who this person that he was looking at, was. Somehow, he felt like he was in someone else's body, staring at someone else's face.

At breakfast the next day, Joe looked across at Anna and said,

"Do you believe in reincarnation?"

Anna looked puzzled and said,

"I don't know, can't say I've ever thought about it."

"Well," said Joe, "In this dream that I had, I died, and I became something else."

Anna stared at Joe.

"What exactly?" she said.

Joe thought for a moment and replied,

"That, I'm not sure of, but I had died, and it was painless. I remember thinking, it never hurt a bit."

It went silent. They looked at each other. You could hear the ticking of the kitchen clock, as they sat at the table drinking coffee. For the first time, they both thought that one day, one of them would be gone and wondered how would the other ever cope?

These things momentarily get stuck in people's minds, usually get shoved to one side, allowing them to carry on peeling the potatoes or mowing the lawn. Sometimes retirement can be more tiring than working; Joe's list of things to be done was endless. Occasionally, he even wished he was building a wall, or putting a floor down for someone, trading banter with his other workmates, even arguing with his son about how to do a job,

then going home tired and having a long hot bath.
In his mind, this idea was far preferable.

Joe was in his greenhouse, on a deck chair. It was early autumn. He still had tomatoes ripening, the smell of which was intoxicating. He also had a grape vine hanging heavy with fruit. Joe felt content. He ate several fresh tomatoes, followed by a few grapes: it was like heaven. The autumn sun was making him squint, as he looked through the glass and watched Anna moving backwards and forwards, as she got the washing in. He smiled and waved. Anna smiled back. Joe leaned back on his deck chair.

For the first time, he started to realise that this is what it's like to be retired. He closed his eyes, he felt free from pain and slipped off to sleep.

Joe woke suddenly, disorientated and feeling sick. He was on the floor, covered in straw and some sticky liquid. He looked up at darkness and saw a single light bulb twinkling like a star. As he stared, he remembered a few moments before, being warm, as he drifted off to sleep in his greenhouse, but now he was frozen stiff. He couldn't quite work out why it was so cold. His thoughts were of that autumn evening, and now it seemed like the dead of winter. For a few moments, he wondered where he had been till now.

As he stared and his eyes got used to the light, he was amazed because he didn't feel pain. He normally felt aches of one form or another first thing, yet it was almost as if he was young again. It then went through his mind that it must be a dream, but somehow it felt very real; the smells were strong, the sounds and feelings stronger, so he came to the conclusion it wasn't a dream.

Then he saw it. This massive head came towards him with an even bigger tongue, which licked him from ear to ear and to there and back. He knew what it was. He had no idea why it continued, as he felt a need to stand. Almost instinctively, he stood, gingerly, wobbly. He looked down at his legs and then realised, "I'm a fucking sheep!" but, to be more precise, a lamb.

He crashed back down to the floor, then got up again. He could feel himself almost dancing to achieve some balance. Eventually he held himself upright. Too many things were now running around in his lamb brain.

He looked around, saw other sheep being born, some even suckling at their mothers. This sight brought on a need to do the same. Only problem was, he didn't want to, apart from the sweat and the shitty smell, he wanted to heave, but his need for food was greater. Before he knew it, he was at the tit, giving it all he could. He loved it, it was rich, it was warm, it was wonderful. Joe felt almost drunk. Satisfied and full, he tottered away to some space, as his mother lay down and gave birth to another lamb.

"Shit!" thought Joe, "I'm going to have a brother or sister."

As he watched, he thought, "What's happening to me? Why am I here?"

He used his uncontrollable legs to wander round the pen, as his mother was attending to the newborn. It was then that a thought came to him.

"Is this what reincarnation is all about?"

The dream he had had, before being here, seemed vivid to him now, but then he thought,

"Surely you're not supposed to know what you were before?"

He didn't know whether to laugh or cry. All he knew was that he wanted some more food, so he made a B line for a spare tit, because his sister or brother was now filling up as well.

Joe was contented; warm, pain-free, he felt as if he had been re-born, which in fact he had been. As he snuggled up to his sister or brother, lying between his mother's legs, he felt affection for both, then pondered his past life. He thought of Anna and the children, but felt nothing; he didn't miss them, nor did he think about whether they missed him.

He thought more, wondering if the other lamb was another person from a past life or maybe even something else. Is this the path of life? Big thoughts for a past builder, even bigger thoughts for a little lamb. He looked up at his mother and fell soundly asleep.

In the coming days, Joe learned that he had a sister. He didn't know how, as there was no real communication, it just came instinctively. Weeks passed. Days of being in the barn were over. Along with all the other lambs and their mothers he was free to roam in the greening fields of springtime.
Joe and his sister Mia (a name he gave to her) were now being suckled by their mother, and also partaking of the lush green grass beneath them. As he quietly munched away, he had never previously contemplated the eating of grass and clover and relishing it, like some sort of super salad. He still thought of his family, but only when he felt fear of something. Up to now all was fine, it was a wonderful life, but somewhere in his mind, he was remembering something, a fact which kept creeping into his head and then vanishing, the moment he was at his mother's tit, or snuggled up warm with Mia.

Joe was in a big open pasture, with all the other lambs. The mothers were dotted here and there. Suddenly he felt aware of danger, as he heard his mother's cries of warning. He and his sister ran as fast as possible towards her for safety. It was almost as if he knew the danger was a fox or a wild dog, prowling nearby. Then he felt it; he knew that, as a person, you fight or flee. As a lamb, you run as fast as you can. You have no defence.

This made Joe feel vulnerable and scared. He thought of his past life and wished he was a human being again, when he would stand tall and maybe chase off the fox or wild dog, or even kill it.

Inside he felt brave; outside he was a baby lamb.

Even when it was pouring with rain, the lambs were in the field.

A late snow would see them being brought back into the barn.

All in all, Joe's contentment was vast. He kept thinking of his pain before, but now he was a spring lamb. He and his sister Mia and their other friends would wander off as far as they thought safe, communicating to each other, and to their mothers, by little bleats and baas, which said,

"How do you feel? Which way? Come back! Leave me alone! let's play!"

Joe understood it all now; like running and jumping, it was automatic, but what he thought about, deep in his mind, he had no idea how to communicate to the other lambs.

Joe and the other lambs loved all the running and jumping, the way little lambs do. Best of all, thought Joe, was just literally throwing himself into the air and landing, then doing it over and over again. All the lambs did it, it was like a rite of spring, the happiness and joy of being alive.

Something was still niggling in Joe's mind, as he cosied up beside his mother and Mia.

"I'm a lamb, so why can't I just be a lamb and not have these thoughts that creep into my head?"

Trouble was, Joe knew somewhere in his mind that things don't go well for lambs or sheep.

Suddenly, he awoke from a terrible dream and realised he needed to communicate with someone or something about how badly it ends for sheep. The penny had dropped. This reincarnation business was shit and it sucked. Specially so for him, as he remembered eating lamb, and that mint sauce was the nicest thing ever to go with roast lamb dinner. Now his mind was panicking.

When Joe woke the next morning, he and Mia were covered in snow, as was their mother, but she was standing and bleating loudly. The late snow had caught the farmer by surprise, despite being aware that the weather can change. Along with his daughter, he was rounding up a small number of scattered sheep; most of the others were already inside the farmer's barn. The farmer called to his daughter,

"Luna, there's two over here with their mother!"

Luna was on an all-terrain bike with a small trailer behind, so she placed Joe and Mia in the trailer with a few other lambs. As the snow wasn't too deep, several of the lambs' mothers followed Luna's bike back to the big barn.

Luna settled the lambs in, followed by the mothers. Each lamb found its mother, all except Joe, who looked around, confused. Luna was about ten years old, had long, blond, plaited hair, stuffed under the hood of her all-weather big coat. She was cute looking, as most ten-year-old girls are. She had also helped to bring most of these lambs into the world.

She knew which sheep belonged where, so she picked up Joe and spoke to him kindly, very much like how you would hold and fuss a puppy. So much so, she seemed taken with him, and he with her; she held him to her, the warmth of her body making him feel secure. It was a wonderful experience for Joe; he nestled into her lap, as she sat on some straw bales, but before long his mother and Mia came over nudging Luna, who said,

"Ok, ok, here's your baby boy!"

For a couple of days, the sheep and their lambs milled around the barn, as the snow slowly thawed, but before it went completely, Joe found himself with Mia at the edge of the barn, where some of the snow had encroached on the straw-covered floor. Joe had forced himself, as he looked down at his hooves, to try and write his name in the snow. He didn't know why, maybe he was subconsciously longing to hold on to what he was before. Mia watched, as he managed to scratch his name and also hers in the snow. Unfortunately, she had no idea what he was doing. She nudged him to play, which he did, but not before Luna had walked towards the barn, to check how the lambs were doing. She stopped in her tracks and looked over one of the pens.

She climbed over and could clearly see the words: Joe, then a gap, then Mia. She couldn't believe it. How was it possible? Joe and Mia were there in front of her. She stared at Joe and his sister, as the other sheep huddled towards the middle of the barn. Joe stared at Luna, thinking how beautiful she was. Her face was bathed in the warmth from the outside lights and with the black sky above, it looked like a kindly moon which had come to rescue him. A second later, full of nervous excitement, she ran off to fetch her dad, who came back with her. It only took a minute or so, but the other sheep and lambs had now moved around the big pen. The words were nearly obliterated; all you could see in the snow was, part of the JO with A at the end.
Luna was annoyed. Her dad looked and said,
"Yes, there's some lines in the snow, and....?"
She looked at him and told him it had said JOE - MIA. Her dad wasn't convinced, so Luna argued and said,
"Who else could have written their names in the snow?"
Luna's dad pulled his cap down over his head and shrugged his shoulders.
"Let's have some tea, it's perishing out here."
Joe looked up at Luna, with all the sadness in his face that he could muster. Luna smiled at him and said,
"Sleep well, Joe!"

Months went by. The sheep were out all the time in the fields, the lambs getting fatter day by day. The farmer was getting ready to send them away to be slaughtered. This was the part of farming which Luna always found hard, as she would always be so attached to the lambs that she had helped bring into the world. This time, however, Luna had begged her dad to spare the two lambs, who were now known as Joe and Mia. Her dad had argued till he was sick, that it was no way to run a farm, but he gave in. Mia would be able to stay and give birth to her own lambs and Joe would be allowed to stay as well. Mia joined the other female sheep as stock, and Joe was allowed to grow up. It wasn't long before they used him as a stud, a job he seemed to take to easily.

Joe felt like a king, a king of sheep. Just by one simple action, he had found a way for him and Mia to survive the cut-throat business of farming and, in lots of ways, he felt content. The thoughts of his past life filtered to the back of his mind and, as he worked at the job in hand, he felt life on the farm wasn't bad at all.

Luna always had time for Joe and even took him to shows, having washed and groomed him, where he even won Best in Show. For him, that was the best. As he made his way round the arena, he held his head high, with the Best in Show label pinned to his horns. You could say he was the happiest he had ever been in this lifetime.

The years flew by, Joe now a mighty-looking ram, who looked the part. Luna, who now ran the farm, was as pleased as punch about how things had turned out, with her dad working fewer hours and often to be found standing against the pen where Joe was kept, admiring him. Nelly, his sheep dog, kept to the right side of the pen; Joe was boss as far as she was concerned.

During this time, Joe often found himself in the fields, where occasionally he would see Mia, but she was getting old now and didn't seem to recognise him. There had been times, just lately, when Joe felt worn out too. Hobbling a bit and with fewer mating sessions, it was as if the clock had turned full circle. He found he could recall the pain he used to be in, in his life before, but now he couldn't take a tablet to ease the pain, although he did get comfort from the attention Luna gave him.

The term "putting out to grass" seemed to apply to him now. Just lately, he'd been thinking about everything, the dreams were getting vivid again and, for some reason, he felt uneasy. As it was late spring, more young lambs were enjoying the sunshine nearby. Joe watched them in an adjacent field, feeling proud. He looked down towards the farm, from the low hill, and, as the sun popped in and out of the clouds, his mind slipped back to being born in the big barn, his thoughts going even further back, to Anna and the kids. As with all memories, he found himself chasing them round more and more; in doing so, he slipped off to sleep.

A warm shower of rain woke him, and a pale sun dried him quickly. He wandered off and found a place under his favourite tree, where he slept again. Just before he woke up, he thought he was talking to Anna, she was telling him to take off his slippers and come to bed. This didn't make sense. He never wore slippers. Then his thoughts shot back to what he was now.
Joe felt tired. When he meandered like this in his head, he got things mixed up.

Then he wondered whether it would have been better to have been born just as a sheep and not have all these memories of another life. He realised that, if that had been the case, he would have been dead many years ago. The tiredness he felt seemed all-consuming almost like he'd found contentment. Joe then closed his eyes as a sheep in a world of peacefulness.

Joe was suddenly woken by a noise which was foreign to him. He couldn't open his eyes, and he felt so hot. Then he felt a rush of blood and an overwhelming desire to stand up, thinking, "Oh no! Not again!"
He struggled to stand up. As he fell over for the third time, his eyes started to clear, realising he was being nudged to stand again. He looked up to see the biggest pair of ears he'd ever seen, and, what's more, a trunk, but on each side of this gargantuan face he was looking at, were the kindest eyes he'd ever seen.

Printed in Great Britain
by Amazon

45080207R00108